Back in the Saddle

MARGUERITE HENRY'S

Ponies *of* Chincoteague

◆ Back in the Saddle ◆

CATHERINE HAPKA

Aladdin

New York   London   Toronto   Sydney   New Delhi

ALADDIN

An imprint of Simon & Schuster Children's Publishing Division
1230 Avenue of the Americas, New York, NY 10020
This Aladdin paperback edition August 2016
Text copyright © 2016 by The Estate of Marguerite Henry
Cover illustration copyright © 2016 by Robert Papp
Also available in an Aladdin hardcover edition.
All rights reserved, including the right of reproduction in whole or in part in any form.
ALADDIN is a trademark of Simon & Schuster, Inc., and related logo is
a registered trademark of Simon & Schuster, Inc.
For information about special discounts for bulk purchases, please contact
Simon & Schuster Special Sales at 1-866-506-1949 or business@simonandschuster.com.
The Simon & Schuster Speakers Bureau can bring authors to your live event.
For more information or to book an event contact the Simon & Schuster Speakers Bureau
at 1-866-248-3049 or visit our website at www.simonspeakers.com.
Book designed by Karina Granda
The text of this book was set in Adobe Caslon Pro.
Manufactured in the United States of America 0716 OFF
2 4 6 8 10 9 7 5 3 1
Library of Congress Control Number 2015957572
ISBN 978-1-4814-5994-5 (hc)
ISBN 978-1-4814-5993-8 (pbk)
ISBN 978-1-4814-5995-2 (eBook)

• CHAPTER •

1

"LOOK–IT'S SNOWING AGAIN."

Haley Duncan followed her friend Tracey's gaze toward the big window at the far end of the crowded school cafeteria. "Yeah," Haley said. "I heard it might today."

Their other friend, Emma, stirred her chili and sighed. "I mean, it's March! Sometimes I think spring will never get here."

"I know, right?" Tracey picked a pale green grape out of her fruit cup and stared at it mournfully. "I swear, when I'm old enough, I'm only going to apply to colleges in, like, Florida."

"Oh, I don't know." Haley watched the fat white flakes

spiral lazily down outside. "I'd miss the snow if I ever moved away from Wisconsin." She glanced at her friends and grinned. "For one thing, it's fun to ride in."

"Riding on the beach sounds fun too," Tracey retorted, and popped the grape into her mouth.

Haley shrugged. "Good point! I bet Wings would like that."

Her smile widened as she thought of her pony, Wings. The spunky Chincoteague technically belonged to a neighboring family, but when their daughter had gone off to college, they'd offered him to Haley on an indefinite free lease. That meant she got to keep him, take care of him, ride him, and treat him as her own pony for as long as she wanted. As far as Haley was concerned, that meant forever.

"Speaking of your riding, when's that big show thingy you keep talking about?" Tracey reached across the table to snag one of Emma's celery sticks. "Maybe Ems and I will come cheer you on."

"Yeah." Emma shivered. "But only if it stops snowing by then."

"It's a week from Saturday." Haley shivered too, but not from the cold. She and Wings had competed in plenty of small, local competitions in her chosen sport of eventing—one-day events, combined training days, and a handful of jumper shows. They'd mostly done well, even winning their share.

Then, the previous autumn, the two of them had taken part in a riding clinic with a well-known advanced-level eventer who was already aiming for the US Olympic Team. It had been a full day of focused learning in all three of the phases that made up the sport—dressage, cross-country jumping, and stadium jumping. Haley and Wings had both learned a lot, and shortly afterward Haley had made a vow to put their new skills to the test by entering a recognized event—one run under the rules of the national governing body for eventing, with licensed judges and fancier prizes. She knew the competition would be tougher there, but she was excited to show what she and her pony could do.

They'd been schooling and preparing for it all winter long, jumping around their homemade cross-country course whenever the snow wasn't too deep, and practicing their dressage and show jumping the rest of the time in the makeshift arena her uncle had plowed for her in one of the pastures. Now, after all that hard work, it was hard to believe the big day was only a little more than a week away!

"The event's a week from this coming Saturday?" Emma said. Haley could see her friend quickly calculating the days in her head, blinking rapidly behind her thick glasses. "Wait, isn't that April Fools' Day?"

Haley shrugged. "I guess so." She took a sip of her juice. "Never thought about that, but yeah, it's April first."

Tracey laughed. "Uh-oh. Hope Wings doesn't decide to play a prank on you, Hales!" Suddenly her eyes widened, and she flicked a grape in Haley's direction. "Heads up!" she hissed. "Hot guys heading our way."

Haley had been smiling, thinking about Wings, but now her mouth twitched down at the corners. *Hot guys?* That sounded like something Tracey's shallow, snooty older sister would say, not Tracey. Well, at least until recently. . . . And what about Emma? A year ago she would have made a joke about that kind of comment, but now here she was tucking a stray strand of hair behind one ear and straightening her glasses as she followed Tracey's gaze with an eager smile.

Trying not to think about how much her friends had changed, Haley glanced that way too. She immediately noticed that one of the three boys wandering toward their table was Owen Lemke, who lived on a dairy farm a couple of miles down the road from Haley's family. He and his friend Vance were kicking an empty soda can back and forth between them like soccer players. Meanwhile the third boy, a skinny kid with a big grin named John, veered around the other two and loped forward to the girls' table. "Hey, ladies. Hey, Ghost Girl." He tugged on Emma's pale ponytail.

"Don't call her that," Haley told him with a frown. Emma had albinism, which meant her skin, hair, and eyes were very pale and her vision was so weak that she was considered legally blind, even though she could see fairly well with her glasses on. When they'd been younger, some of the other kids had teased Emma for being different. Haley had been in lots of confrontations—and even a fistfight or two—while standing up for her friend, and so had Tracey. But over time Emma's happy disposition had won over most of the other kids, and she didn't get teased much anymore.

"It's okay." Emma giggled and slapped John's hand away from her hair. "I don't mind."

By now Owen and Vance had reached them too. "Yeah, chill out, Haley." Owen grinned at Haley in that cocky, irritating way he had. "You seem kind of tense. Did your runty little mutt pony buck you off into a snowbank or something?"

"No way," Tracey put in loyally. "In fact, we were just talking about how Haley's totally going to rock this big show she's doing soon."

"Really?" Owen raised one eyebrow. "Let me guess. Does it involve a postage-stamp-size saddle and tight sissy pants?"

Vance snorted with laughter. "Yeah. And lots of prancing and fancy braided manes and stuff."

Haley just rolled her eyes in response. Most of the other horse people in this rural corner of Wisconsin rode

Western, usually on registered quarter horses, paints, or Appaloosas. For instance, Vance was one of the top junior ropers in the area. Owen didn't compete in roping, though he sometimes entered his horse, Chance, in other Western events at local shows and rodeos.

John reached over Emma's shoulder, grabbed one of her cookies, and shoved it into his mouth before she could snatch it back. "That's okay," he said as he chewed. "Haley's probably better off sticking to the sissy English stuff."

"True, true." Owen puffed out his chest. "If you can't ride with the big dogs, best stay on the porch."

Tracey let out a snort. "Oh, please. Haley could ride rings around you dummies."

"Oh yeah?" Owen grinned. "Then maybe she should prove it. There's a penning at River Ranch this weekend. If you're so hot, Duncan, maybe you should come show us how it's done."

"Thanks, but no thanks." Haley sipped her juice. "Wings and I are getting ready for an important event. We don't have time for that kid stuff."

"Kid stuff?" John hooted. "Ooh, burn!"

Owen kicked at the leg of Haley's chair, almost making her lose her grip on her juice glass. "Sure, that's what they all say when they know they can't keep up," he taunted. "I know the real reason you don't want to come. You know I'll make you and that spotted little thing you ride look like sissy English losers."

"Right, that's totally it." Haley put as much sarcasm into her voice as she could. "Actually I'm worried that your fat, lazy horse might accidentally break into a trot or something, and fall over from the effort. If Wings is in the way, he might get smushed."

Tracey giggled. "Good one, Hales!"

Owen just snorted. "Seriously, Duncan. What are you afraid of? Think all that jumping and prancing you've been doing made your pony forget how to be a real cow horse?"

"What's to remember?" Haley shrugged. "Even a dummy like Chance can remember how to do something like that."

She felt a twinge of guilt as soon as she'd said it. It was one thing to make fun of Owen, or to point out the obvious fact that Chance wasn't as quick or lively as Wings.

But Chance was a nice enough horse in his own way, and it wasn't his fault he belonged to such an annoying owner. Or his fault that Haley couldn't help comparing him to the world's smartest, most perfect pony.

"She probably thinks she's too good for a penning," Vance drawled. "Those English riders are like that, you know."

"Yeah," John put in with a laugh. "They'll only go riding with, like, the queen of England or something."

"With tea afterward," Vance added, crooking one pinky finger as he pretended to sip tea.

Tracey giggled. "I so can't picture Haley having tea with the queen!" She shot Haley a sheepish glance. "No offense, Hales."

Haley ignored her, glaring at all three boys. "Anyway, I don't have time for playing silly cowboy games right now, okay?"

"Don't have time, or don't have the guts?" Owen countered. "Five bucks says you're just making excuses because you know you can't beat me."

"Oh yeah?" Haley perked up at the mention of money.

The entry fees for recognized events were a lot more than the fees for local schooling trials, and after paying for this event, she didn't have enough money left over for the new saddle pad she'd been eyeing. Maybe this penning was a way to make sure she and Wings looked their spiffiest for the big day. . . .

Then she shook her head. She could do without that new pad—she and Wings wouldn't need it to do their best. It was more important to stay focused on their goals.

"Bwack, bwack!" Owen danced around with his hands tucked under his armpits, flapping his elbows like wings. "Duncan's a chicken!"

"Chicken, chicken! Bwack!" The other two boys started dancing and clucking along.

Haley gritted her teeth as kids at nearby tables started turning around to see what was going on. "Stop it, you weirdos," she snapped. "I'm not a chicken."

Owen stopped dancing, though the other two continued. "Oh yeah?" he challenged. "Prove it. Come to the penning and show us what you've got."

Haley hesitated, thinking over her schedule. She'd

planned to do a dressage schooling on Saturday, followed by some trot sets and hill work on Sunday. Then again, maybe Wings didn't need more drilling in dressage. He'd been going really well lately. Why not reward him with something a little more fun than endless circles and transitions? A little cross training might be exactly what the pony needed to keep him on his toes. Not to mention being exactly what Haley needed to wipe that infuriating smirk off Owen Lemke's face.

"Okay, you're on!" she blurted out, almost before she realized what she was saying. "We'll be there. Prepare to be humiliated."

Owen grinned. "Ditto."

"Anybody home?" Haley hollered as she stepped into the front hall of her house. She paused to kick off her school shoes, which were dusted with snow.

There was no answer, which wasn't much of a surprise. Haley's parents had died in a car crash when she was four, and she'd lived with her aunt, uncle, and two older cousins ever since. The whole family managed to eat breakfast and dinner together almost every day, but those meals were often the only time when all five of them were home at once. Uncle Mike worked part-time as a pharmacist and full-time running the family farm, which had long since switched from dairy cows to hay, organic vegetables, and hunting leases. Aunt Veronica was a freelance computer programmer who was always on the go. Seventeen-year-old Jake had a part-time job and was on the baseball team at school, while thirteen-year-old Danny spent most of his spare time tinkering with the robots he liked to build and playing a rotating variety of sports.

After grabbing a slice of bread and an apple from the kitchen, Haley headed up to her room, thinking about the penning this weekend. Had it been a mistake to say she'd do it? Her big event was less than a week and a half away, and there was still a lot she wanted to do to prepare.

"Too late now," she murmured as she dropped her schoolbag onto the bed. If she backed out of the penning, Owen would probably tease her about it until the end of time. Or at least until the next time she and Wings kicked his butt at some Western play day or other, which might be weeks from now.

But so what? Haley thought as she bit into the apple. What did she care what stupid Owen Lemke said about her? He was only doing it to get under her skin because he was totally obnoxious.

Of course, that wasn't what Tracey thought. For some reason she seemed to think Owen liked Haley—as in, *like* liked her. Which was crazy, in Haley's opinion. But she'd just about given up on convincing Tracey of that. Tracey and Emma had both gone boy crazy this year, focusing way too much on clothes and makeup and shopping and way too little on anything useful or interesting. Sometimes Haley worried that she didn't have much in common with her best friends anymore.

Well, her local best friends, anyway. As she finished the apple and reached for her battered paddock boots, her gaze fell on the laptop poking out of her schoolbag. She wanted to get a ride in before it was time to start her evening chores. But it was staying light later every day now, and she figured she had enough time to take

• 13 •

a peek at the Pony Post before she headed out to get Wings.

The Pony Post was a private website that the four members had created to make it easier to share their interest in Chincoteague ponies. In addition to Haley, the members were Maddie Martinez, Brooke Rhodes, and Nina Peralt. Maddie lived in Northern California and rode a cute pinto mare named Cloudy at her local lesson barn, where she always seemed to be trying something new, from painting her patient pony's hooves to riding out through the vineyards in the surrounding hills.

Brooke had saved up her money to buy her pony, a young flaxen chestnut mare named Foxy, at the annual pony auction in Chincoteague, Virginia. Haley had known Brooke—online, at least—for almost two years now, but she still could hardly believe the other girl had actually attended the one-of-a-kind event made famous in Marguerite Henry's classic book *Misty of Chincoteague*.

Then there was Nina, who kept her pony, Bay Breeze, at a stable in the middle of New Orleans. She was a dancer and an artist as well as being a rider, and her stories of life in the big city sometimes seemed like something out of a book or movie.

Haley knew she didn't have much in common with the other girls when it came to the places where they lived and the things they did when they weren't at the barn. But that didn't matter. They all shared the love of their ponies, and that would never change.

Soon the familiar site logo appeared. Haley quickly logged on and scanned a couple of new entries from Brooke and Maddie. Brooke was home from school already, since she lived in Maryland, where it was an hour later than it was in Wisconsin. Maddie was on California time, two whole hours earlier than where Haley lived. Haley was surprised to see that the new photo Maddie had shared of her pony had been posted just a few minutes earlier.

Haley opened a new text box and started to type.

[HALEY] Hi, guys! Maddie, did u skip school today? Why r you posting now?

She sat back and waited to see if Maddie was still online. A few seconds later a new post appeared after hers:

[MADDIE] Hi, Haley! No, I'm here—study hall. Totally booooooooring. Luckily Ms. Q doesn't care what we do as long as we're quiet, hehe, so I'm just catching up on my 'net time!

[HALEY] Lucky u, we're not allowed to go online in school unless it's for homework. But as long as ur here, I could use ur advice. I think I might have done something stupid today.

[MADDIE] Uh-oh, what?!?

Haley's fingers flew over the keyboard as she explained what had happened with Owen. When she finished, she posted it and once again sat back to wait for Maddie's response.

It came a few moments later.

[MADDIE] Team penning looks like a blast! U should totally do it!!!!

[HALEY] I know, it's fun, Wings and I have done it lots before. But it might not be the best time right now, u know? It's only about a week before our event, and we should be practicing dressage, or working on sharpening up our show jumping, or even doing more trot sets to make sure we're as fit as we can be.

[MADDIE] U have been working so hard all winter, tho! U are so ready—u could use a break!! Besides, who says u can't practice your dressage at the penning, right?

[HALEY] Huh? I don't think they'll let me set up a dr. ring in the pen, lol! Besides, the cows might get in the way!

She grinned as she posted it, picturing a bunch of excited heifers crashing through the little white chains that a lot of people used to mark out their dressage rings, or stampeding in at *A* and running right over the other letters that were always set up around the outside of the ring.

Then she blinked as another response from Maddie popped onto her screen.

> [MADDIE] Don't be a goof, you goof! I'm talking about PRACTICAL dressage!! Isn't a dressage test just mostly steering and accuracy? That's what Ms. Emerson always tells us in my lessons, anyway. Riding a straight line, doing sharp transitions, making proper turns and circles, yadda yadda . . . You'll get to practice all that stuff in a new, distracting setting, which can only help prepare u for that big event, right?

Haley grinned as she read over Maddie's post a second time.

> [HALEY] M, u are a genius! I never thought about it that way. But don't tell Owen, OK? I can just

picture what he'd think if I ever told him that he and Chance were actually doing practical dressage. . . .

She and Maddie chatted for a few more minutes until Maddie's study hall was over. Then Haley logged off, still smiling at the thought of Owen doing dressage without even realizing it. Glancing at the window, she noticed that it had started snowing lightly again. Her smile grew.

This could be one of my last chances to ride in the snow this year, she told herself as she quickly pulled on her boots. *Better get out there and do it!*

Soon she was in the wide barn aisle tightening the girth while Wings, who was in the crossties, shifted around and snorted and generally acted as if he didn't want to stand still another second. Her favorite dog, Bandit, twined around her legs, panting eagerly.

"Okay, okay, just let me finish tacking up." Haley paused to give the rangy collie mix a pat on the head. "Don't worry. You can come with us."

She was glad that she'd planned for today to be a

conditioning day. Even though trot sets and hill work were a necessary part of their training, since they helped keep Wings fit enough to complete a long day of eventing, that work could be a little boring. It would be much more fun doing today's ride in the snow.

A couple of chickens wandered into the barn, feathers fluffed against the wintery weather. They squawked in alarm when Bandit leaped toward them, barking.

"Stop it, you naughty boy!" Haley exclaimed, but she couldn't help laughing as the dog trotted back over to her, looking quite pleased with himself.

The hens recovered quickly, strutting back into the barn and scurrying through the tack room door, which Haley had left ajar when she'd fetched her saddle.

"No, no!" Haley dashed after them and shooed them back out into the aisle before they could leave their messy droppings all over everything. Then she grabbed her bridle off its hook and headed back out, glancing around to make sure no other birds, cats, or dogs had sneaked in while she hadn't been looking. She pulled the door shut behind her and returned to Wings, whistling "Let It Snow."

A few minutes later she led the pony out into the flurries, tipping her head up to catch a few flakes on her tongue. Bandit trotted along beside them.

"Ready to go, boys?" she asked pony and dog as she pulled down her stirrups.

She swung into the saddle and clucked to start Wings walking, using her legs to steer him around the side of the barn toward the back gate, which led to a barren hay field and the woods and meadows beyond. The wind tickled her cheeks, making her shiver a little, but she was smiling. Wings felt happy and eager to go, Bandit was frisking along with his usual good cheer, and Haley had all sorts of fun stuff to look forward to in the next couple of weeks. After Maddie's pep talk, Haley couldn't wait to wipe the smug look off Owen Lemke's face by beating him at that penning. And after that, of course, came the big event.

"Get used to winning, Wingsie," she whispered, kicking the pony into a brisk trot. "Because we're going to be doing a lot of it!"

◆ CHAPTER ◆

2

"BRR!" UNCLE MIKE SAID AS HE SWUNG OPEN the heavy rear door of the family's small stock trailer. "It's a chilly one this morning!"

"What else is new?" Haley smiled as she glanced inside the trailer, where Wings stood beside a stout liver chestnut quarter horse. When her cousin Jake had heard about the penning, he'd decided to tag along and enter the fourteen-to-eighteen competition. They'd pulled into the local ranch that was hosting the day's event, to find the parking area already more than half full of trucks and trailers.

Both horses were loosely tied in the trailer. Being tied kept the horses from moving around too much while the rig was in motion. Jake was already at the front untying Rusty from the outside. "Heads up. He's coming out," he called, reaching in through the trailer's slats and slinging the lead rope over the gelding's beefy neck. Then he clucked. "Back, boy."

Rusty ducked his head and backed carefully out of the trailer, lowering one hind foot over the drop and then the other. As soon as all four feet were on the ground, he lifted his head and pricked his ears toward the big covered arena nearby. A small herd of heifers was penned at one end, mooing and milling around restlessly. Rusty let out a snort and took a step toward them, ears still at full attention.

"Whoa, big fella," Uncle Mike said, reaching forward to grab the dangling lead rope. "I've got you."

Jake hurried around to take the horse from his father. "He's okay. It's just been a while since he's been to a penning."

Haley nodded and looked around. It had been a while for her, too. A couple of years ago she and Wings had attended team pennings and sortings as often as they could, though once she'd gotten more serious about eventing, she'd cut back on other competitions. There were still plenty of familiar faces in the crowd—some from school, some from past pennings. A few trailers down, an older girl waved at her before going back to running a brush over her Appaloosa gelding's broad, spotted hindquarters.

Haley waved back, her heart jumping with anticipation. She was glad Maddie had helped talk her into coming today. This was going to be fun!

"Okay, let's get this show on the road," Uncle Mike said. "You going in to grab that pony of yours, Haley, or you want me to do it?"

"No, I've got it." Haley jumped into the back of the trailer, talking soothingly to Wings. He tended to be a little more excitable than the family's placid quarter horses, and after the last time he'd bolted and led them all on a merry chase around the parking area of an event, he wasn't allowed to back himself out anymore.

Haley reached his head and untied the lead, then let out a cluck. Wings was small and agile enough to turn around easily in the two-horse stock trailer once the other horse was out, and it was a lot easier to lead him out that way. Soon they were both jumping down onto the hard-packed dirt of the parking lot, which had been completely cleared of snow.

"Hey, you made it!" Owen hurried over, dressed in cowboy boots and jeans with a big belt buckle. He grinned at Haley. "Thought you might chicken out after all."

"Not a chance." Haley busied herself straightening Wings's halter, not wanting Owen to think she cared what he thought. "I wouldn't want to miss out on showing you how it's done."

Uncle Mike chuckled. "How you doing, Owen?" he said. "Still got that nice big bay gelding of yours?"

"Yes sir, Mr. Duncan." Owen smiled politely. "He's going better than ever."

Haley's uncle smiled back, then wandered over to close the trailer door. Rusty had settled down by then and was standing quietly as Jake saddled him. But Wings was still alert, jigging at the end of his lead rope. Suddenly he let out a shrill whinny, almost yanking the lead out of Haley's hand as he whipped his head around to watch a big raw-boned chestnut jog past.

"Easy, buddy," Haley said, bumping him with her

elbow to stop him from crashing into her as he spun around to stare the other way.

Owen blinked at the pony. "Uh, he seems kind of freaked out," he said. "Maybe he's feeling insecure about being a runt pony in a horse's world."

Haley scowled at him. "He hasn't been anywhere new in a while, that's all," she said. "Anyway, I think it's kind of nice that he's more interested in his surroundings than some dull old stock horse who never notices anything."

She grimaced as a cow bellowed in the distance and Wings spun in that direction, almost knocking into her again. It was true what she'd told Owen—the only times Wings had left the farm since the clinic last autumn had been for lessons at her eventing instructor's farm, where he'd been tons of times before. Maybe it was good that they were getting used to going to new places again before the event next weekend.

Just then Haley spotted Tracey and Emma hurrying toward her. Tracey was wearing designer jeans and a pink cowboy hat, while Emma had an American-flag-printed bandana knotted around her neck.

"Surprise!" Tracey exclaimed breathlessly, skidding to a stop in front of Haley. "We're here!"

"Hi, Wingsie," Emma added, reaching out from a safe distance to give the pony a careful stroke on the nose. She was a little nervous around horses, though she always tried to be a good sport about it. Wings snuffled at her briefly, then returned to staring around.

"You're here," Haley echoed. "I thought you guys were going to the mall today to get free makeovers or whatever."

"You fell for that?" Tracey grinned and slung an arm around Haley's shoulders. "Come on. You know we'd never miss being here to cheer you on." She turned her smile in Owen's direction. "Hey, Lemke. What's up?"

"Not much," Owen said. "See you guys later, okay? I have to check on my horse."

As he hurried off, Emma leaned closer to Haley with a smile. "We're mostly here to cheer you on," she whispered. "But partly for the cute cowboys, too."

Haley smiled, though her stomach twisted a little at the reminder of how much her friends had changed. Cute cowboys? Seriously?

Uncle Mike hurried over, saving her from responding. "Better go sign in," he told her. "I'll hold Wings for you."

Haley nodded and handed over the lead rope. Uncle Mike had a calming, easy way with horses—and people, too, for that matter. He would help Wings settle, if anyone could.

"Be right back," Haley told her friends, diving into the crowd.

At the sign-in table Haley paid her fee and got her team assignment. It turned out she'd be riding with a girl she knew a little who was a year ahead of her in school, plus a sandy-haired boy she didn't recognize.

"Hi, I'm Kenny," he introduced himself when the organizer called him over.

"Haley," Haley said. "Nice to meet you."

"I'm Tia," the older girl added, taking in Kenny's well-worn jeans and boots. "You done much penning? I haven't seen you here before."

Haley winced at the challenge in Tia's voice, but she listened with interest for Kenny's response. It would stink if getting stuck with some newbie made her look stupid in front of Owen.

"It's my first time here, but not my first time penning," Kenny replied. "I just moved here from Minnesota. I've been penning since I could ride, and riding since I could walk."

Haley let out a breath of relief, then traded a grin with Tia. That sounded promising, especially since he'd said it in such a matter-of-fact way that she was pretty sure he wasn't just bragging.

"Cool," Haley said. "Welcome to Wisconsin, then. Let's get our horses and get warmed up."

Kenny's eyes widened slightly when he saw Wings, but he didn't say anything. His own mount was an older quarter horse mare with wise eyes and a crooked blaze.

Tia mounted her flashy paint gelding and surveyed the little herd of heifers, which someone had just released into the pen. "Looks like the cows are pretty fresh," she commented.

Haley nodded, snugging up the cinch on her Western saddle. The cows were bleating and practically running over one another as they moved around the big pen. Wings snorted as a bald-faced heifer bounced off the metal fencing nearby.

"Easy, boy." She mounted quickly, then lowered a hand to his withers, giving him a rub. "We'll get our turn at them soon enough."

"Talking to animals again, Duncan?"

Haley didn't have to turn her head to know that it was Owen. He'd just ridden over to the rail, looking comfortable atop his compact but muscular quarter horse.

"I was just telling Wings how we're going to kick your butt, Lemke," she retorted.

Tia laughed. "You said it, Haley!"

Owen rolled his eyes. "Here I thought maybe you were telling him what a real horse looks like."

"Whatever." Haley glanced over her shoulder as she heard someone call her team. "We're up, guys!"

She felt a shiver of excitement as a woman swung open the gate, letting Haley and the rest of her team into the pen.

After that, things happened fast. The announcer called out three numbers, and Haley and her team had to find the cows wearing those numbers and separate them from the herd.

"Heads up, Haley," Tia called out. "Got a seven over to your left."

Haley glanced that way and spotted the heifer Tia meant, a big-eared one with a stubborn expression.

"Okay, Wings," she murmured. "Let's show our stuff."

She didn't dare look around to see if Owen was watching as she sent her pony toward the cow. Wings jigged, clearly wanting to speed up, but Haley kept him at a walk. If they scattered the herd, it would take forever to get them back.

The cow eyed the pony as he got closer, and finally scooted away in the direction Haley had hoped she would. Wings was watching the cow now, ears pricked.

"Easy, easy," Haley murmured as they pressed the heifer a little harder, trying to aim her toward the far end of the arena. "That's the way . . ."

The cow snorted and tried to duck past to return to the herd, but Kenny scooted in and blocked her. When number seven turned back and took off at a lope, Haley and Wings were ready. The pony leaped forward, staying close beside the cow to keep her separated from her herd mates.

Kenny was right there too. Meanwhile Tia had galloped to the far end and was waiting to help corner the cow and then keep her there while her teammates fetched the other two they needed.

By the time the three of them had pushed all three heifers into the small pen and raised their arms for the timer, Haley was breathing hard and smiling from ear to ear.

Top that, Lemke, she thought, finally chancing a look around at the spectators. She saw Tracey and Emma waving at her, and she waved back, glad that she'd come. Maddie was right—she and Wings had needed to let off some steam and have a little fun.

Haley was still in a good mood the next afternoon as she saddled her pony for a ride. "Okay. We missed our dressage schooling yesterday," she told Wings, who was standing quietly in the crossties for a change, watching the chickens running up and down the barn aisle. "So we should do at least a little dressage today and then go ahead with our trot sets."

She hummed as she tightened the girth another notch,

then gave the pony a pat on the shoulder. Her team had just edged out Owen's yesterday, winning first place in their age group. Tracey and Emma had been excited, jumping around doing little cheers. Owen had come over and congratulated her, but he hadn't been able to resist joking that the cows had probably mistaken Haley's spotted pony for one of them.

"Whatever, Lemke," Haley had said, feeling a bit smug as she'd brushed the sweat marks from Wings's coat. "You're just jealous because you wish you had a pony who could do anything."

She'd expected another joke, but Owen had just shrugged. "I guess he's okay, for a runt pony. Anyway, we'll get you next time."

"We'll see." Her smile had broadened. "But first Wings and I have something more important to do—win that event next weekend!"

In the Sunday afternoon quiet of her home barn, Haley felt a shiver run down her spine as she thought about what she'd said. Just six days until she and Wings made those words come true!

"Come on, boy," she said. She led the pony into a nearby field and then swung into the saddle. "Let's do some dressage."

Most of the previous week's snow had melted, revealing the clear spot Uncle Mike had plowed in the deeper snow for Haley's dressage ring. She glanced toward it and nudged her pony's sides, but he stayed where he was.

"Come on, Wingsie," she said. "Walk on."

She clucked and asked again, and finally Wings stepped off into a walk.

Haley chuckled. "Okay. I know you don't like dressage that much," she said, "but we have to do it. Eventing is about more than just running and jumping, you know."

Wings flicked an ear back at the sound of her voice, but didn't respond when she nudged again with both legs to ask for a trot. Haley was surprised.

"Are you okay, buddy?" she said. "Come on, let's go!"

She kicked harder, and Wings picked up a choppy, sluggish trot. Haley bit her lip, wondering if they'd overdone it the day before. What if Wings had used up all his energy at that penning? What if this hurt their chances at the event?

Uh-oh, she thought. *Did I make a big mistake?*

Haley always gave Wings the day off on Monday, just like many of the big-time trainers did. On Tuesday she hurried home from school, and barely paused to wolf down a banana before heading out to the barn. Wings had perked up after a while on Sunday, but his energy had remained lower than usual. What if he was still tired today?

He seemed a little more like his normal self in the crossties, shifting his weight and snorting at Bandit as the dog wandered past. Still, Haley was nervous as she gave him a quick grooming and then fetched her saddle. If the pony was still tired, would they have to scratch from the event? It was only four days away, and there didn't seem to be much point in going if she knew they wouldn't be at their best. . . .

But when she mounted, Wings leaped forward, trying to break into a trot as soon as Haley's rear end hit the saddle. She smiled with relief as she pulled him up.

"Hey, settle down," she chided, though she didn't really mind his antics this time. "Glad you're feeling better today, but we've got work to do."

That evening after dinner Haley logged on to the Pony Post. She scanned the latest entries, smiling at some new photos Nina had posted of Breezy. Then she opened a text box.

[HALEY] Good news, guys. Wingsie's back! He was raring to go today, ha ha! Lucky it was a XC day b/c I think he would've exploded if I'd tried to make him do dressage!!! As it was, he overjumped everything I pointed him at by like a yard, lol! Soooo glad that penning didn't tire him out too much after all! Whew! But yeah, we had a great ride today, and I know we're ready for the big day on Sat. Ready to win, that is!!!

◆ CHAPTER ◆
3

THE REST OF THE WEEK PASSED IN THE BLINK of an eye. At least that was how it felt to Haley as she emerged, yawning, from the cab of Uncle Mike's truck into the cool morning air on Saturday. She stretched and looked around, her sleepiness evaporating instantly when she got a look at the scene before her.

The event was taking place at a stable about forty minutes' drive from her house. It was the same farm where she'd attended the clinic in the fall, and once again she was impressed by its immaculate twin barns, large riding rings, and acres of rolling hills, which managed to look lovely and manicured despite the dusting of snow that lingered in the shadier spots. Horses and riders were everywhere, some of the horses still dressed in stable blankets, some tacked up and ready to go, many somewhere in between.

Haley had received her ride times a couple of days earlier. She checked her watch and saw that she had at least two hours until she needed to start warming up for her dressage test. Good. That would give Wings plenty of time to settle in.

"Let's get you unloaded." Uncle Mike checked his watch too as he hurried toward the trailer. "I need to get back for my shift at the drugstore."

Haley nodded. "Thanks for bringing me," she said. "Don't worry about what time you get back here this afternoon. I don't mind hanging out and watching if we're finished before you come to get us."

"Okay." The corners of Uncle Mike's eyes crinkled as he smiled and gave her shoulder a squeeze. "Sorry I can't stay and watch."

"It's okay. Jan will be here." Haley glanced around, wondering how she was ever going to find her trainer in this crowd.

Jan Whipple was a successful local event rider who ran a busy lesson-and-training program out of her small farm a few miles from Haley's home. Several of her other students were also competing in this event, and she'd assured Haley's aunt and uncle that she'd look after Haley and Wings while they were there.

Wings was on his toes as he jumped out of the trailer and got a look at his surroundings. "Good boy," Haley said, tugging on the lead to remind him she was there. "Does this place look familiar?"

The pony let out a snort, lowering his head to sniff at a patch of half-frozen mud. Meanwhile Uncle Mike was unloading Haley's tack trunk, a big plastic box on wheels that held her jumping and dressage saddles along with everything else she was likely to need.

"Let's find Jan," he said, pulling out his phone. He sent a quick text.

The phone beeped a few seconds later. "Where is she?" Haley asked, keeping one eye on Wings, who was still on high alert.

Uncle Mike rubbed his mustache and squinted off to

the left. "Said to aim toward the grove of pines near the dressage ring," he said. "Must be thataway. Come on. Let's go."

Haley followed, leading Wings, as her uncle pulled the wheeled trunk along through the rutted parking area. When they passed the pine trees, Haley spotted Jan a dozen yards away brushing a tall, lanky bay horse tied to a trailer.

"There she is," Haley said, waving to the trainer.

Jan waved back, and a moment later a teenage boy emerged from behind the horse and hurried toward Haley and her uncle. "You made it!" he said with a shy but sincere smile.

"Yep," Haley said. "Andrew, this is my uncle Mike. This is Andrew—he rides with me sometimes in my lessons at Jan's."

Haley had first met Andrew at the clinic last fall. His horse was the one Jan was currently grooming, a talented but green young thoroughbred he'd bought at the racetrack. Andrew was on an even tighter budget than Haley was and had been doing most of Turbo's training on his own, but when Haley had told him about Jan, he'd started taking lessons with her whenever he could afford it. Both he and his horse had responded beautifully to Jan's training, which was why she'd encouraged them to enter this event.

"Nice to meet you," Andrew said with a bashful nod at Uncle Mike. "I can take that trunk the rest of the way if you want. Jan said you're in a hurry."

"Thanks, son." Uncle Mike consulted his watch again. "I should get going. Haley, you going to be okay?"

"Sure," Haley said. "Thanks. I'll see you later."

Uncle Mike hurried off in the direction of the rig. Haley waved, feeling a tiny twinge of disappointment. It had been fun having family and friends around to share her win at the penning last weekend. But nobody from her family was able to come and watch the event today, and her friends were busy too—Emma with a family birthday celebration and Tracey with a trip to Chicago with her sister.

But she didn't dwell on that for long. There was too much to do!

◆ ◆ ◆

Half an hour later Haley was walking the cross-country course with Jan. While horses weren't allowed to see the jumps before they competed, it was customary for riders to hike around the course on foot to plan out the best way to ride each obstacle. Haley always loved getting a close-up look at the jumps. For one thing, walking a course always gave her ideas for new jumps to build at home!

Andrew was along for the course walk too. So was the other student who would be riding at their level, a boy Haley's age named Kyle. Haley had ridden with him in a few group lessons over the past year or so, though she didn't know him that well, since he went to school in a neighboring district. His horse, Augie, was an older buckskin gelding with a kind, quiet temperament—Jan called him "a good egg." Augie struggled a bit with show jumping but was reliable and brave and always willing to try. He reminded Haley of the steady paint mare she'd ridden in lessons when she'd first been learning to jump at age seven or so. Kyle himself was just as cheerful and likable as his horse, with wavy reddish-brown hair that always seemed to be sticking up, and a broad, freckled face that always seemed to be smiling.

"Wow, this is so exciting!" Kyle exclaimed as they approached the first fence, an inviting log surrounded by mulch. His eyes widened as he glanced from the log in front of them to a larger one immediately to its right, and then an even larger one beyond that. "Wait, which one is ours?"

Jan chuckled. "The small one," she told him. "Don't panic. As I told you, there are several levels competing this weekend, but the three of you are doing beginner novice."

Haley nodded along with the others, though she couldn't help glancing at the next biggest log, which she knew had to be for the novice-level competition. She'd already completed a couple of unrecognized events at that level, but Jan had convinced her to drop back to beginner novice for her first recognized event. Now that she saw the jumps, though, she almost wished she'd pushed harder to stay at novice.

Wings and I could totally handle that log, she thought, barely listening as Jan talked to them about how to ride the obstacle. Her gaze wandered over to the biggest log. *In fact, we'd be able to kill the training one too—easy peasy!*

She did her best to forget about that. It was too late to switch levels now. But if she and Wings won, Jan would have to let them move up next time, right? That was just one more reason to make sure they did their very best today.

By the time Haley and the others had finished the course walk, the earliest riders in their division were already performing their dressage tests. "Should we watch a few?" Andrew asked as Jan hurried off to check on one of her higher-level adult riders. "None of us needs to get tacked up for a while, right?"

"Sure." Haley led the way over to the rail of the big dressage court. Inside, the organizers had set up a couple of dressage rings marked off by chains and a series of letters. There was enough space left over for a judge's table at the end of each ring, plus an area around the outside of the chains where riders could warm up just before their tests. Like everything else about the dressage phase, the ring setup was very detailed and exact. Haley had measured out her own makeshift dressage ring often enough to know the dimensions and letter placement by heart. The ring was supposed to be exactly twenty meters by forty meters, and the seemingly random letters set up around the outside followed a precise order—*A, K, E, H, C, M, B, F.* There were lots of mnemonic phrases people used to help them remember that order, but Haley had been eventing long enough that she didn't need one anymore.

When Haley and the boys arrived, a woman in her twenties was just finishing her test. As the young woman left the ring, a girl a couple of years older than Halcy rode in on a tall, gorgeous liver chestnut mare with an arched neck and an elegant head.

"Wow, nice horse!" Kyle commented to Haley and Andrew as the girl rode past at a brisk trot, looking totally focused on her riding.

"Yeah." Haley watched the horse start her warm-up, impressed by the way the mare moved—more like a fancy dressage horse than a lower-level eventer. The girl looked good too. She sat the mare's big trot easily, her back straight and her legs never moving.

Haley felt a quiver of nerves. This pair was in her

division? Wow. She and Wings were really going to have to be at their best to beat a team like that!

But we can do it, she told herself as a bell rang, signaling for the girl to begin her test. *We can do anything!*

The team performed just as beautifully as they looked like they should, turning in a smooth test with prompt transitions and tidy circles. Their only bobble came on the turn up the center line at the end. Haley could see that the girl was anticipating the end of the test, and she cut the corner short and was a little crooked when she reached the middle of the ring. But she managed to correct within a stride or two, and their halt and salute were crisp and professional-looking.

Haley clapped politely along with the other spectators. "Hey, nice job," Kyle called to the girl as she rode out of the gate. "I like your horse."

"Thanks." The girl halted outside the ring, looking down at Kyle and the others. "Athena's a star." She gave the mare a quick pat on the withers.

"I'm Kyle, and this is Andrew and that's Haley." Kyle pointed to each of them. "We're in this division too."

"Yeah. Looks like your score should be the one to beat," Andrew added with a soft chuckle.

The girl smiled briefly. "Thanks. My name's Riley. Do you guys compete at this place a lot?" She shot a look around. "It's pretty nice."

"First time competing here," Haley spoke up. "What about you?"

"Me too." Riley loosened her reins, and her mare dropped her head and sniffed at Kyle's shirt. "I live down in Iowa, but this event got good reviews, so I figured we'd give it a try."

"Iowa? Really?" Haley was surprised. The state line was hours away!

"Yeah." Riley shrugged. "I'll travel anywhere in Area Four to compete, just about. We did our first beginner novice in Illinois, and I competed on my old horse as far away as North Dakota."

"Wow." Kyle looked impressed. "You must be really experienced."

"I guess." Riley shrugged again. "Athena and I will probably move up to novice next time out. We almost did it this time. If I'd known how easy the cross-country course was going to be, I would have."

"Cool," Kyle said.

Haley didn't say anything. Riley hadn't sounded as if she were bragging. Not really. But her comment still bothered Haley a little—as if the older girl already considered herself too good for the rest of the people in her division. As if she already assumed she was going to win.

Not if I have anything to say about it, she won't! Haley thought fiercely.

"Look, next rider's starting," Andrew said, nodding toward the ring as the judge's bell tinkled to signal the start of the next test.

Haley turned to look. The rider entering the dressage ring was a nervous-looking middle-aged woman, and the horse a chunky draft cross. Haley winced as the pair almost turned the wrong way on their first turn, and then corrected awkwardly and almost bumped into the little chains marking the edge of the ring.

"Whoa," Kyle murmured. "That was close."

Haley nodded. Stepping out of the ring meant automatic elimination—not just from the dressage test but from the whole event. She held her breath as the pair veered crookedly through their twenty-meter trot circle.

Haley had memorized the test so well that she barely had to think about what came next—left lead canter depart between *K* and *A*. At least that was what was supposed to happen. Haley could see the rider kicking frantically as her horse pounded at a rapid trot past the flag marking *K*, and then the one at *A* as well. They'd almost reached *M* on the next long side when the horse finally lumbered into a ponderous canter on the wrong lead—and plowed right through the chain at the end of the ring.

"Oh no!" Kyle exclaimed with a groan.

The buzzer went off as the woman, red-faced and embarrassed-looking, wrestled her horse around.

"Sorry, sorry!" she exclaimed breathlessly as a man—her trainer, Haley guessed—hurried out to grab the horse's bridle and lead the pair away.

Haley averted her eyes as they passed, trying not to imagine how humiliated the woman must feel. "Poor thing," Haley whispered to the boys once the woman had moved off. They watched as several volunteers rushed over to fix the chain the horse had knocked askew.

"Yeah, bummer for her." Kyle grinned. "But good for us, right? One less person we have to try to beat!"

Andrew laughed, and Riley let out a snort. Haley had almost forgotten the older girl was still there behind them.

"Whatever," Riley said. "See you guys later. I'd better get Athena cooled out."

"Bye," Kyle called, and Andrew added, "See you."

Haley didn't say anything, watching as Riley rode off and disappeared into the crowd. Once again Haley found herself a little annoyed by the other girl. What had that snort meant? Had it been just a reaction to Kyle's silly comment, or had it meant that Riley didn't think the woman on the draft cross was any real competition for her, whether the woman was still in the competition or not? Either way, Haley knew it would be awfully satisfying to beat Riley and her big, fancy horse. . . .

"Come on," she said, glancing toward the trailer where Wings and the other horses were tied. "We should probably go start tacking up. It'll be our turn soon."

⋆ CHAPTER ⋆
4

"GOOD BOY, WINGS." HALEY PATTED HER pony. "We can do this."

They were outside the ring waiting for the rider before them to finish her dressage test. Haley took a few deep breaths, trying to quiet the butterflies fluttering around in her stomach. She rarely got nervous when she rode, but she was nervous now.

Jan was standing beside her, watching the previous rider, but she looked up at Haley's comment. "You *can* do this, Haley," the trainer said, giving Wings a rub on the shoulder. "Just relax and remember to use all your space and don't let Wings rush his transitions.

You get that stuff down, you'll do fine."

"Thanks." Haley shot her a small smile. She wanted to do better than "fine," but she didn't bother to say so. Jan already knew that Haley always rode to win.

As the previous rider snapped out her salute, Haley gathered up her reins. Wings had warmed up well, and he seemed to be completely over his travel jitters. She ran through the test in her head, reminding herself to ride into the corners and watch that final turn up the center line. Wings might not have as fancy a trot as Riley's mare, but judges always seemed to like him. She and Wings could beat everyone if they did their best—even hotshot Riley from Iowa.

The previous competitor rode out. She was a confident-looking woman in her fifties on a big Appaloosa gelding. "Good luck," she called to Haley as she walked past on a loose rein. "Cute pony, by the way."

"Thanks." Haley nudged Wings forward, rode through the gate, and aimed around the outside of the chain while she waited for the judge's bell. She still felt a little jittery but tried to swallow it down.

"Go, Haley!" Kyle called from the rail. He and Andrew

were both sitting out there on their horses. Andrew had taken his turn in the ring right before the woman on the Appaloosa. Turbo had spooked at a leaf blowing outside the ring, messing up one of the trot circles, and both of his canter transitions had been a little early. Otherwise they'd done well, and Haley knew Andrew was proud of his horse.

But he didn't come into this expecting to win, she told herself. *Wings and I can't make any mistakes at all if we want to beat Riley.*

She shortened her reins another notch, pushing her pony forward into a working trot. As she rounded the far end of the dressage ring, she heard the tinkle of the bell.

"Time to go," she whispered to Wings, turning and heading for the entrance to the dressage ring.

As they entered at *A,* Haley looked straight forward toward the judge's table behind the letter *C.* Wings felt good beneath her, forward and focused.

Here we go, she thought as they trotted up the center line for the first time. *What's that thing Nina always says? Aim for the stars?*

That made her think about the Pony Post. Had she remembered to check in with them that morning as she'd promised?

As she tried to think back, she realized Wings was almost at the other end of the ring already. She quickly closed her leg and pulled on the right rein for the turn, then realized they were supposed to turn left at *C*, not right.

Oops! she thought, quickly correcting. Wings tossed his head, a little surprised, but obediently veered to the left.

Whew, that had been close. Haley felt her cheeks turn pink as she realized she'd almost made the same mistake as that nervous older woman earlier. That wasn't the way to win.

She didn't make any more big mistakes after that, but her concentration had been blown by the near disaster, and even as she swept into her salute at the end, she knew it hadn't been their best ride. She kept a smile on her face until they turned away from the judge, then blew out her breath in a whoosh, slumping in the saddle as she exited.

"Nice ride," Riley said as Haley passed.

Haley shot her a look, wondering if the older girl was being sarcastic. But Riley had already turned to watch the next rider enter.

Jan hurried over to meet Haley as she rode away from the ring. "Well done, Haley," she said. "Saw your bobble at the beginning, but you recovered well." She patted Haley on the knee, then gave Wings a rub on the neck.

"Thanks, but we definitely could've done better," Haley said.

"You can always do better." Jan raised an eyebrow at her. "If not, why even bother competing?"

"Yeah, I guess," Haley muttered.

Just then a woman over by the results board called Jan's name, and the trainer looked that way. "I'd better see what she wants," she told Haley. "You okay?"

"Sure." Haley forced a small smile, and Jan hurried away.

Andrew dismounted and led Turbo over to where Haley and Wings were standing. Kyle rode after him. "Good job, Haley," Andrew said. "Your transitions were really accurate."

"Thanks, but I know we messed up." Haley sighed, giving Wings a pat. "It was totally my fault. I spaced out when we came in and, well . . ."

She let her voice trail off. Kyle shot her a sympathetic smile. "It's okay," he said. "You know you're still going to beat me by at least fifty points."

Haley smiled weakly as Andrew chuckled. Beating Kyle wasn't what she'd had in mind for today. Her gaze wandered back to Riley, still standing ringside.

Andrew followed her gaze. "I know that Riley girl looked good in dressage," he said. "She'll probably win this phase. But who knows if that fancy horse of hers can even jump, right?"

"Yeah." Haley felt a twinge of hope. It was true—there were still two phases yet to come.

"You and Wings always kill the jumping phases," Kyle reminded her cheerfully. "Especially cross-country. That's what Jan says, anyway."

"It's true," Andrew told him. "I mean, you've seen them in lessons. Wings is a cross-country machine!"

Their comments made Haley feel a tiny bit better.

Because they were right. There were still two phases left in the competition. Two phases that happened to be the ones she and Wings were best at. She'd never come out on top in dressage in her life, and that hadn't stopped her from winning in the past. In fact, she'd never failed to improve by several places by the end of the day, since at least some of the top dressage performers usually had faults in the jumping phases.

"I just wish we'd been able to show what we can really do," Haley said. "We've been working so hard in dressage, and all it took was one tiny mistake to throw us off, you know?"

"That's eventing for you." Andrew squinted toward the ring. "Hey, Kyle, better get back over there. Aren't you next?"

Kyle pulled a slip of paper out of his pocket and consulted it. "Nope. There's two more after this one before it's my turn."

"That must be one of them." Haley watched a girl around her own age riding toward the ring. Her horse was an attractive and kind-eyed bay mare with four white socks.

"Hey, I know her," Andrew said. He waved as the girl passed them. "Good luck, Claire!"

The girl, Claire, glanced down at him briefly. "Thanks," she said without slowing down.

Soon she was in the ring beginning her test. "How do you know her?" Haley asked Andrew.

"She rides with a trainer I took a few dressage lessons with before I started going to Jan," Andrew said. "She'd just started when I was there last summer, actually. She'd been riding for a couple of years but was brand-new to eventing."

Haley watched the mare round the far turn and begin her first trot circle. "Her horse has a fancy trot," she commented.

Both boys nodded, and they all watched in silence for a moment. The bay mare's gaits were lovely and steady, and the rider wasn't making any major mistakes. However, Haley couldn't help noticing that their circles weren't exactly round, and a few of the transitions were early or late.

At least that's one more rider Wings and I will probably

beat, Haley thought, trying to make herself feel better about her own ride.

When Claire rode out of the ring, she paused to talk to her trainer, a lean man wearing a sweatshirt with a stable logo on it. Then she rode over to Haley and the others.

"It's Andrew, right?" she said, glancing at Turbo, who was grazing on a bit of winter-brown grass. "Is that the same horse you had before?"

"Uh-huh." Andrew gave the thoroughbred a pat. "He's come a long way, right?"

"I guess." The girl glanced at Haley and Kyle. She had bright blue eyes and a sharp chin. "Hi. I'm Claire."

Haley and Kyle introduced themselves. "Nice ride, Claire," Kyle added.

"Thanks." Claire smiled rather smugly. "My trainer says Bella always wins the dressage. She used to compete at intermediate before I bought her."

"Really?" Haley knew that intermediate was the second-highest level in eventing. No wonder the mare was so fancy!

"Yeah, her owner was maybe going to try her at

advanced, but my dad made him an offer he couldn't refuse, because I just had to have her." Claire patted her horse. "Come on, Bella. Let's go celebrate with some nice carrots, hmm?"

She rode off without saying good-bye. "She's . . . interesting," Kyle commented.

"I don't know her that well. But I heard that her family is pretty rich," Andrew said.

Just then Jan bustled over. "Heads up, Kyle," she said briskly. "You're on deck, so look alive."

"Okay." Kyle shortened his reins, waking his horse from what appeared to be a quick nap. "Here goes nothing!"

Forty minutes later the last of the beginner novice riders had finished their dressage tests, and the judge's scribe was shuffling through some papers, standing in front of the big wooden bulletin board near the ring. Haley and her teammates watched from a polite distance, Haley's fingers crossed in the pocket of her breeches as she waited, more or less patiently, for the scribe to post the dressage scores. Had the judge noticed her mistakes? If so, how much would it bring down her score?

"Okay, they're up," she told Andrew and Kyle as the scribe finally pinned several sheets to the board. "Let's go check out the damage."

Haley hurried over, with the boys on her heels. Her heart sank when she immediately spotted Riley's name at the top of the list. She scanned down, hoping hers would be right below it. And down, and down . . .

"I got eleventh." Andrew sounded delighted.

Haley glanced at his name, then finally spotted hers a couple of spaces below. "Thirteenth for me," she said, trying not to sound as disappointed as she felt.

"There's me, number twenty-two," Kyle said cheerfully. "Hey, at least I beat a few people!"

"Including the one whose horse jumped out of the ring and got the big E," Andrew joked, giving Kyle a playful punch on the arm.

"Hey, I'll take what I can get," Kyle retorted with a grin.

Haley couldn't muster a contribution to their banter. Instead she just stood there staring at her name. Thirteenth place? That was pathetic. How was she supposed to win the division after a start like that?

Unlucky thirteen, she thought with a grimace. *Is the universe playing an April Fools' Day prank on me?*

"Ow," she blurted out as someone pushed past, knocking her aside and almost stepping on her foot.

"Excuse me, excuse me!" It was Claire, bullying her way to the front of the group of riders gathered around the results. She scanned the list of names and scores and let out a gasp. "Ninth place? *What?*" she exclaimed. She whirled and scowled at Andrew as if he were somehow responsible for her results. "But we did *much* better than that, don't you think?"

"That's eventing for you," Andrew replied philosophically. "You win some, you lose some."

Claire frowned at him. "Bella doesn't lose," she snapped. "At least she shouldn't, not after how much Daddy paid for her!"

She stormed off without waiting for a response, almost bowling over an elderly man as she went. "Wow," Kyle said. "She seems kind of bummed about her score."

"Yeah." Haley was a little annoyed that Claire had beaten her, though she guessed the mare's fancy gaits might have had something to do with it. But Haley did her best to shake that off. Claire wasn't her competition—Riley was. And Haley was going to have to stay focused if she wanted to make up enough ground to beat her. "Come on," she told the boys. "Let's go find Jan and give her the news."

Jan was back at the trailer helping an adult student tack up her horse. She nodded at the news about the scores.

"Okay, so now you know what you need to do on cross-country," she told Haley, Kyle, and Andrew. "There's nothing out there you and your horses haven't seen before, so just ride your plan and think forward. It's a nice, flowing course, and you can all do it."

"I know Augie can do it," Kyle joked. "I just hope I can hold on for the ride."

"Don't be silly," Haley told him. "You'll do great." She was already feeling the thump-thump-thump of excitement inside her as she thought about the course. Jan was right—it was nothing she and Wings couldn't handle in their sleep. Doing some quick calculations in her head, she figured out that Riley would have to incur only a couple of jumping faults and maybe some time penalties, and Haley would be breathing down her neck by the time they hit show jumping.

And all Wings and I need is to get close, she thought fiercely, *and we'll be able to psyche Riley out and win!*

◆ CHAPTER ◆
5

THE START BOX FOR CROSS-COUNTRY WAS in a broad, sunny field with a view of most of the rest of the course. Haley glanced out, mentally riding the whole course as she waited for the starter to count down her time.

Log to roll top to brush to coop, she thought. *Then we'll have to be careful at the ditch. Jan thought it might ride a little funky if the sun's too bright and the horses have trouble getting a good look at it. . . .*

Since the course was essentially a big loop around the property, the finish line was just a few yards off to one side of the start box. As Haley circled Wings, making sure he was on the aids and paying attention, a man galloped in on a sweaty chestnut horse.

"Whew, that was fun," the rider exclaimed to no one in particular. He brought his horse down to a walk, gave it a hearty pat, and then glanced over at Haley. "Watch out for the brush near the beginning," he called to her. "It's easy for them to want to stop right after coming up that steep hill."

"Thanks," Haley responded absently. She'd just spotted Riley hand-walking her horse around in circles while chatting on her cell phone. The older girl had just finished her cross-country course, and Haley couldn't help wondering how she'd done. Haley squinted, trying to read the expression on Riley's face—excited? content? maybe a little disappointed?—but the girl was too far away.

"Ready?" the starter asked, holding up his watch. "Ten seconds."

"Ready. Thanks." Haley rode into the box and turned around, keeping a tight hold on the reins so Wings wouldn't burst out early. Out of the corner of her eye, she watched Riley fiddle with her horse's bridle.

". . . three, two, one," the starter said. "Go!"

Snapping back to her own ride, Haley urged Wings forward. He was ready, leaping out of the box and almost immediately surging into a brisk canter.

"Easy, easy," Haley murmured, sitting up and half-halting to bring him back a little. Wings was fast, and Haley never worried that they'd get time faults for going too slowly. But at beginner novice level, you didn't get any extra points for going faster than everyone else. In fact, you would be penalized if you came in too far below the opti-mum time.

The first obstacle was just a few strides away now. Wings pricked his ears and sailed over the big, round log jump easily. Haley just caught a glimpse of the jump judge giving her a thumbs-up from her lawn chair beside the log, before the judge fell out of view as Wings cantered off toward the next obstacle.

"Good boy," Haley murmured.

She glanced forward at the roll top coming up halfway across the flat field. But it was still a good distance away, and as Wings cantered easily down a slight hill, Haley's mind wandered to Riley again. Haley wished she'd had enough time to find out how the other girl had done. Then she'd know exactly what she needed to do.

Wings jumped the roll top perfectly out of stride. After that the course veered off to the left, along a dirt trail through a small grove of trees, and then up a steep hill leading up to another big, flat field alongside the dressage and jumping rings.

"Go on, Wingsie," Haley muttered, feeling the pony's gait falter ever so slightly as they neared the trees. The bare branches formed a lattice of shadows on the hard-packed dirt below, and Wings was giving the odd-looking footing a hard look.

But a kick and a cluck were all it took to send the brave pony forward again. Soon they emerged from the shadows and faced the steep hill. Wings attacked it eagerly, and Haley glanced at her watch to see how they were doing on time so far.

Except she immediately realized, with a stab of dismay, that she'd forgotten to start the timer on the watch while she'd been in the box!

Oh, man! she thought. *I was so busy worrying about Riley that I totally spaced.*

Wings surged over the lip of the hill, and Haley blinked, forgetting about her watch as she saw the brush jump coming up fast in front of them. Yikes! No wonder that man had warned her about this one. It had looked like an easy five strides when she'd walked it with Jan and the others earlier. But Wings had decelerated as soon as he'd crested the hill, staring off toward the horses and spectators over by the rings, and she'd be lucky to get to the jump in six strides with enough impulsion to make it over.

"Get up, Wings!" she cried, giving him a stout kick with both legs. "Keep moving, buddy!"

The horse snorted and surged forward. But at the same time he shook his head and humped his back as if thinking about tossing in a buck.

"Quit!" Haley growled, booting him again.

He leaped forward but stumbled, lurching forward and scrabbling to stay on his feet. He recovered quickly and cantered on, but Haley instantly realized that the stumble had really messed up their striding. They were going to meet the brush on an awkward half stride. The jump wasn't that big, and Wings should still be able to make it over if she could convince him to take the long spot. . . .

She kicked frantically, but Wings had had enough. He tossed his head again and skidded to a stop right in front of the jump.

No, no, no! Haley thought frantically, already adding the points for the refusal onto her dressage penalties. Out of the corner of her eye, she saw the jump judge make a note on her score sheet.

She pulled Wings to the side and kicked him into a brisk trot before turning toward the brush jump again. Wings pricked his ears forward, then pinned them back and started to slow down.

"Go, go, go!" Haley cried, reaching around to tap him behind her leg with her crop.

Wings let out a grunt of surprise—Haley rarely had to use her crop on him—and shot forward. He met the brush jump at an awkward spot again, but this time he kept going, leaping up and over the brush jump but twisting in the air to keep his front legs from hitting it. He landed hard on the far side, and Haley felt herself flying through the air. . . .

Oof. She landed on her left shoulder and rolled onto her back. "Rider down!" the jump judge cried into her radio, leaping to her feet. She was a fortyish woman with a motherly look about her. Soon she was on her knees beside Haley. "Don't try to move yet, dear."

"I'm okay," Haley said breathlessly. She rolled into a sitting position and looked around for Wings. He hadn't gone far before stopping to nibble on a shrub off to the side of the course.

"I've got to get my pony," Haley said. But as she struggled to her feet, legs shaking, she saw someone dart out from the spectators and make a beeline for Wings. It was Kyle. He grabbed the pony's dangling reins and led him toward Haley.

"I'm sorry, dear," the fence judge said, patting Haley on the arm. "I'm afraid this means you're out."

"I know." Haley's heart sank as she accepted what had just happened—how everything had gone all wrong in the blink of an eye. She'd fallen off, and she knew what that meant. The big E. Elimination.

She moved forward to meet Kyle and Wings. At the same time Jan appeared out of the crowd and dashed over.

"Haley! Are you okay?" the trainer cried. "What happened? Did you hit your head?"

"No, I'm fine." Haley flexed her left arm just to make sure. "Landed on my shoulder."

"Okay." Jan still looked worried. She glanced at Kyle. "I'll take Wings," she said. "Thanks for catching him."

"You're welcome." Kyle glanced at Haley, as if expecting her to thank him as well.

But Haley didn't say a word. She couldn't. The disappointment had just hit her, far more painful than the minor bumps and bruises she'd sustained in the fall. Her event was over. Not only had she failed to win, but she hadn't even completed. There would be no show jumping for her and Wings later. No ribbon. No enjoying the look on Riley's face when Haley beat her.

How could this have happened?

"How does this look on me?" Kyle grabbed the light blue tenth-place ribbon hanging on a clothes rack near Jan's trailer and held it up against his shirt like a tie. Haley looked up from folding coolers and stuffing them into a trunk.

Andrew grinned and grabbed the ribbon out of the other boy's hand. "Hey, give it back," he said. "Turbo and I earned that thing fair and square!"

"I know, I know," Kyle said with a laugh. "Who knows? Maybe Augie and I will get our own ribbon someday. In about a billion years. If I'm lucky."

"You can have mine if you want a stupid ribbon so much." Claire sounded grumpy as she tossed her own brown eighth-place ribbon at the boys. She was leaning against the next trailer, watching Jan's group pack up. "It's definitely not the color I was expecting."

"Wow, sore winner much?" Kyle murmured into Haley's ear as he hurried past with an armful of saddle pads to add to the trunk in front of her.

Haley just shrugged. Yeah, Claire was acting like a brat, but Haley couldn't really blame her. Haley wasn't in the best of moods herself after what had happened earlier. She still couldn't believe that she'd messed up so badly. And the worst part? It had totally been her fault. Eventing was all about guts, preparation, and focus. She'd started that cross-country course with plenty of the first two. But she realized now that she hadn't really been focused from the start, and it hadn't taken long for that to catch up with her.

The other worst part was that she'd had to hang around for the rest of the day watching the others have fun. Riley had ended up winning the beginner novice division, of course. Her mare had floated over the show jumping obstacles as if they'd been six-inch crossrails, never coming close to touching any of them.

Andrew and Kyle hadn't done as well, though both of them seemed pleased enough with their performances. Turbo had gone clear cross-country and had knocked down one fence in show jumping, which had been enough for that tenth-place ribbon. Kyle had done fine on cross-country, with just a few time faults, but as usual Augie had been sloppy in stadium, knocking down more jumps than he'd left standing. Kyle and Augie had finished well out of the standings, though Kyle seemed pleased just to have completed the event, and he couldn't stop bragging playfully that he hadn't come in last this time.

Jan poked her head out of the trailer, where she'd just gone to put something in the storage area. "Your uncle called, Haley," she said. "He's on his way to pick you up. Should be here in twenty minutes."

"Thanks," Haley muttered without looking up from the trunk full of coolers.

Jan stepped out of the trailer, pocketing her phone. "Hey," she said, walking over to Haley. "You still down in the dumps over that fall? That's not like you. Shake it off, girl, and start thinking about next time."

"Easy for you to say," Haley snapped before she realized what she was saying. Out of the corner of her eye, she saw Kyle and Andrew trade a wide-eyed look. Jan was pretty easygoing, but she wasn't one to tolerate a lot of back talk.

The trainer just sighed, though. "Listen, Haley," she said briskly. "You win some, you lose some. That's eventing, right?"

"I guess." Haley stared at the square of fabric in her

hands. "But Wings and I have made it over way harder stuff than that stupid brush thing."

"Sure you have." Jan shrugged. "But this time you didn't. It happens."

"Only when I mess up," Haley countered. "And I definitely did. Big-time." She finally met Jan's gaze square on, practically daring her to say it wasn't true.

Jan's frank blue eyes met Haley's without blinking. "Okay," the trainer said. "Maybe you did mess up. But the footing was tricky on the landing from that jump, and the approach coming so soon after the hill was giving people fits all day. Who knows how much was you and how much was the course, right? Either way, you've got to learn from it and move on. Doesn't do any good to beat yourself up."

This time Haley just nodded and looked away. No matter what anyone said, Haley knew it was her fault they'd been eliminated. Wings was as sure-footed as they came; he wouldn't have stumbled if she'd been paying attention to the footing. It wasn't like him to stop either, no matter what kind of distance they found. If she'd ridden more aggressively, he probably would have jumped the first time. And maybe if she'd been sitting back more, she wouldn't have come flying off over his shoulder like a beginner when he had finally made it over that fence.

Yes, this was all her fault. She'd let her pony down, and she'd let herself down. There were no two ways about it.

She glanced at Wings, who was standing tied to the trailer with the other horses. Turbo was nibbling at the hay net Andrew had hung for him, and one of the other horses kept trying to chew on her lead rope. But Wings was standing quietly with one hind leg cocked, looking sleepy. Haley couldn't help flashing back to that first ride after the penning, when he'd felt sluggish and a little tired. How much had the exciting day chasing cows taken out of him? Was that maybe the real reason he'd stumbled out there? Was he still a little tired and sore from the unaccustomed movements of playing cow pony?

Maybe, she told herself. *But never mind. It's not going to happen again. Because next time I'm going to make sure we're ready. I'm going to make sure we redeem ourselves. Big-time.*

"Hey," Kyle said, breaking into her thoughts. "You okay?"

Haley blinked up at him, forcing a smile. "Yeah, just thinking about the future, like Jan said," she told him. "And listen, thanks for catching Wings for me earlier."

"Oh!" Kyle flashed her a smile. "Sure, anytime, Haley. No big deal."

"Still." Haley glanced at Andrew, who was fiddling with some tangled reins nearby. "Sorry I've been kind of a grump today. It was fun seeing you two do so well, anyway. Congratulations."

"Thanks." Andrew traded a look with Kyle. "And don't worry, Haley. You and Wings will get 'em next time."

Haley nodded, her chin jutting out with determination. "I know we will. Definitely."

By nine o'clock that evening Haley was so exhausted that she could hardly keep her eyes open. She ignored a couple of e-mails from Tracey, deciding she could wait until tomorrow to hear all about her friend's trip to the big city. But she stifled a yawn and logged on to the Pony Post, knowing her friends there would be waiting eagerly for an update on her event.

> [HALEY] Hi, guys. Well, today didn't go quite like
> I'd hoped. . . .

Her fingers raced over the keys as she poured out the whole story. Well, the important parts, anyway. She figured she could fill in the details tomorrow.

After she finished and posted the message, she scrolled back to see what the others had posted that day. Only a few seconds passed before she heard the ping of a new message posting.

> [MADDIE] O, Hales, sorry about the E! Total
> bummer. But it happens, right? Just do what I did
> the time I accidentally scored for the other team
> in a soccer game—put it behind u and pretend it
> never happened, ha ha!

[HALEY] Lol. But ur right, I already have a plan to put it behind me.

[MADDIE] Good! What's the plan?

[HALEY] That girl Riley I mentioned? She said she'll be back in this area in 2 wks. There's an unrecog. event where she's going to try moving up a level. Said she wants an easy first course before she tackles novice at a recog. one.

[MADDIE] 2 wks? That seems soon!

[HALEY] Ya, her horse is rly fit tho. And Wings will be fine too, since he barely even did anything last time.

[MADDIE] Wait, what??

[HALEY] Ya, that's what I was gonna tell u. I already e-mailed in my application for the BN division at the same event. That's when Wings and I are going to show everyone what we can RLY do!!!!

She smiled as she hit the button to post the message. Yes, that was her plan, all right. At least she'd only have to wait a couple of weeks for her redemption.

• CHAPTER •
6

HALEY LEANED ON THE STALL DOOR WATCH-
ing her pony eat his breakfast. Behind her in the barn aisle
a chicken squawked loudly, and Wings lifted his head and
stepped to the door, dribbling grain over Haley's arm as
he stared out.

Haley frowned, glancing from Wings to the grain
raining down onto the floor, and back again. "Hey," she
said. "I just realized you haven't had your teeth done in a
while. How long has it been, anyway?"

By then the pony had lost interest in the action in the
aisle and returned his attention to his bucket. But Haley
wasn't really watching him anymore. She was staring into

space, trying to remember the last time the equine dentist had visited. Last year around Memorial Day, was it? Or had it been longer than that?

She spun on her heel and hurried down the barn aisle, dodging the cat lounging in the middle. Bandit had been sniffing around the feed alcove, but he barked and dashed after her as she raced across the barnyard.

"Sorry, boy. Can't come in," Haley said breathlessly, nudging the dog back with the toe of her boot as she let herself through the white picket gate leading into the backyard.

Moments later she was in her aunt's home office at the back of the house looking through the little book of addresses and phone numbers she kept in her desk. Living out in the country as they did, her aunt and uncle insisted on having all important numbers written down on paper in case they needed them in an emergency when the power was out and computers and cell phones couldn't help. Haley was glad, since her own laptop was all the way upstairs and she didn't dare touch Aunt Veronica's computer without permission.

"Equine dentist, where is it?" Haley muttered, paging past numbers for various relatives, neighbors, and farm-related business contacts.

Finally she reached the page where her uncle had scrawled numbers for various vets, farriers, and other professionals who worked on their animals. Halfway down the list was Steve Harasta, the local equine dentist.

Haley grabbed the phone and dialed the number, then tapped her foot impatiently as she listened to it ring. Moments later a groggy voice answered with a mumbled "Hello?"

"Oh." Haley gulped as she realized it wasn't quite seven a.m. yet. She was so used to farm life—getting up early, doing chores, and riding before school—that she hadn't stopped to think that not everybody woke up with the sun. "Um, sorry to call so early. This is, um, Haley Duncan? From out on Dairy Road?"

"Mmpf. Right. How are you, Haley?" The dentist sounded slightly more awake with each word. "How can I help you?"

"It's Wings." Haley clutched the phone, glancing

toward the window, which had a view of the barnyard. "I think his teeth might be in pretty bad shape."

"Oh yeah?" Now Steve sounded fully alert. "What happened? He have an accident or something?'

"No, nothing like that. It's just, he's been dropping a lot of grain without chewing it lately. And at our event over the weekend, he wasn't quite himself. I was thinking the bit might have been bothering his mouth."

Actually, Haley hadn't really been thinking that until about five minutes ago. But the more she thought about it, the more sense it made. It wasn't like Wings to refuse a fence, or to stumble, either. What if he'd been off his game because his mouth was sore? Horses' teeth were always growing, and if the dentist didn't file off the sharp points now and then, it could cause big problems. Sure, Wings had seemed okay on their rides since the event, but it had only been a few days.

"Okay," the dentist said. "Guess I could come take a look. I think I have some openings week after next, or—"

"No!" Haley blurted out. "I mean, couldn't you fit us in earlier than that? It might be an emergency."

"Might be?" Steve sounded amused. "Well, all righty then. Let me just check my book and see what I can do. . . ." There was a long pause. Haley held her breath and crossed her fingers until the dentist spoke again. "Okay, hold on. Looks like I could squeeze you in day after tomorrow—Friday. It'll have to be late, though— say, four thirty?"

"Perfect!" Haley grinned with relief. She didn't want to think about how she would have managed to deal with an appointment during school hours. "We'll see you then."

Two days later Haley watched as the dentist finished his work. Steve was a big man with broad shoulders and huge biceps, but he had a light touch with horses. As usual, Wings had been suspicious at first when the dentist had brought out the speculum, an enormous, shiny metal contraption that held a horse's mouth open so the dentist could reach to the back teeth without risking a bite. Haley had been ready to step forward and help, but Steve had talked softly to the pony until Wings had let him slide the speculum into place.

After that, Steve had pulled out various files and other instruments, humming cheerfully as he'd worked in the pony's open mouth. Haley had been surprised at how quickly the dentist worked. Before she knew it, he was carefully pulling the speculum back out, to Wings's obvious relief.

"How were his teeth?" she asked. "Pretty bad?"

"Nope. Pretty good, actually. Wasn't much for me to do." Steve dropped the speculum into a stainless steel bucket and swished it around in the cleaning solution. He winked at her. "Definitely not an emergency."

"Oh." Haley glanced at her pony, feeling sheepish. "Well, it just seemed like maybe the bit might be bothering him."

"Doubt it, unless there's something wrong with the bit." Steve peeled off his gloves. "His teeth are fine."

"Oh." Haley's heart sank. She looked over all her tack every time she cleaned it, so she knew there was no problem with her bit. So if it hadn't been the pony's teeth, that meant she still needed to figure out the reason for their poor performance.

"Always good to keep on top of things, though," Steve added with a smile. "Just call if you need me again."

"Okay. Thanks." Haley handed him the check her uncle had left, then watched him hurry back out to his truck.

When he was gone, she gave Wings a pat and a couple of carrots. Hearing a flurry of barks from the tack room, she remembered that she'd locked Bandit and one of the other dogs in there to keep them out from underfoot. When she released them, the big yellow Lab immediately trotted off toward the food dishes farther down the barn aisle. But Bandit rubbed against her legs like a cat. Then he dashed over and grabbed the knotted rag Haley had given him as a toy. He dropped it at her feet, wagging his fringed tail hopefully.

"Sorry, boy," Haley said. "No time to play today."

She rubbed the dog's head, then let Wings out of his stall and led him outside. Halfway across the big pasture the family's other horses were already grazing on the first soft shoots of spring greenery poking up from among brown winter-killed grass and patches of lingering snow. Letting out a whinny, Wings took off as soon as Haley released him, throwing in a couple of playful bucks as he ran toward the little herd. Chico kept eating, but Rusty and Jet looked up at the pony's approach, and Rusty even snaked his neck and ran with Wings for a few strides before returning to grazing.

Haley smiled as she watched her pony play. "Guess you're feeling pretty good after your dental appointment," she murmured.

Back in the house she went upstairs, planning to get a head start on her homework before it was time to set the table for dinner. When she opened her laptop, though, she couldn't resist checking in on the Pony Post first. There were a couple of new messages:

[MADDIE] Study hall check-in! Ugh, why do Fridays seem to last twice as long as any other day? Well, the school part anyway, lol! B, cute pix of Foxy, she sure is furry! Cloudy doesn't grow that much of a winter coat, maybe b/c Ms. E puts a blanket on her whenever it goes below like 50 degrees, ha!

[NINA] Hi, all! Sorry I didn't check in yesterday, we ended up going out to eat. But my lesson after school was great. Did I already tell u guys my friend Avery switched to my lesson day? She's been riding w/Jordan and me for a few wks now. Fun! We got to do some jumping today, and next time we're going to ride out thru the park maybe. What have u all been doing w/yr ponies? Brooke, is Foxy still shedding like a fiend, ha ha? And, Haley, how's Wings doing? Did the dentist come to check his teeth like u said?

Haley scanned both of her friends' chatty messages, but she barely took in most of what they'd said, even though she normally would have teased Maddie about her barn owner's California blanketing habits. She was still too focused on Wings to think about anything else. She opened a new text box and typed quickly.

[HALEY] Hi, guys! Ya, Nina, the eq dentist just left. He said W's teeth were fine???? I don't get it. If it wasn't that, what could it have been?????????

[NINA] Haley! Hi, I'm still here!

Haley was surprised when Nina's new comment popped up beneath hers. She hadn't even noticed that her friend's last message had posted just a few minutes earlier.

[HALEY] Hi! So what do u think? I don't know what to do next to fix W's problems!

[NINA] Hmm. Are u sure he has probs?

[HALEY] What do u mean? There has to be some reason we messed up so much at the event. B/c we were soooo ready!! Esp. since we only did BN level. I mean, we should be able to rock that stuff in our sleep! Esp. on XC!!!!

[NINA] Yeah. But maybe it was just the spirit of April Fools' Day messing w/u! Ha ha ha ha!

[HALEY] ☺ Very funny. I guess it could've been that penning after all. I should have known better than to work him so hard only a wk before the big event, ugh! He was prob a little sore from all the sliding stops and quick turns and stuff. I won't make that mistake again.

[NINA] OK. But don't be too hard on yrself or Wingsie. Stuff happens, right?

Haley grimaced. She admired Nina's easygoing approach to life most of the time, but this was different. If Haley couldn't figure out why they'd done so poorly at that event, it might happen again. She already knew why their dressage score had been so low, and all she had to do to fix that was make sure she knew her test inside out and didn't get distracted. But the jumping stuff was another matter. . . .

[HALEY] I guess. But I think I'll have the farrier out early to check him. Come to think of it, that would make more sense, right? If his feet weren't quite right, it might make him stumble. . . . Grr, too bad I didn't think of that sooner—I have a lesson on Sunday.

[NINA] A lesson? Cool! Are you going to yr trainer's farm?

[HALEY] Yep. It's a group lesson to work on show jumping. That's good, since W and I didn't even get to do that part at the event, grrr!

[NINA] Sounds good. Oops, my dad just got home—gtg. Let us know how the lesson goes!

[HALEY] U know I will. Bye!

She logged off and stared at the blank screen of her laptop. Normally she loved it when she ended up chatting live with one or more of the other Pony Posters. With their busy lives in three different time zones, that didn't happen very often.

But today she almost wished Nina hadn't been online. Because her comments hadn't been very helpful. In fact, Nina hadn't seemed to take Haley's problem very seriously at all!

Then Haley shrugged and pushed herself to her feet. She could try to explain it to her Pony Post friends better later. Right now she wanted to go call the farrier before she got caught up in her homework and forgot.

"Hold still, you wiggle monster," Haley chided with a laugh. Even though his head was mostly immobilized by the crossties in the barn aisle, Wings had managed to swing his body away from her as she'd tried to sling his bright purple cooler over his back. "You need to wear this until you're dry."

It was Saturday afternoon, and she and Wings had just finished a dressage schooling session. Afterward the pony had been pretty sweaty under his winter coat, so

Haley had sponged him off and then scraped and rubbed him as dry as she could. But he was still damp, and there was a chilly wind that day, so she'd fetched the cooler to help him dry the rest of the way before she turned him out.

Finally the pony held still long enough for her to get the cooler on and buckled. Then she unclipped him from the ties and led him to his stall, where she'd already dumped an armful of sweet-smelling hay.

"Go on, have a snack while you dry," she told him with a smile.

The pony didn't have to be told twice, diving into the hay pile with gusto. Noticing a pile of manure in the back corner of the stall, Haley hurried to fetch a fork.

When she dumped the manure into the wheelbarrow parked in the alcove, she saw that it was almost full. With a groan she decided she might as well go dump it now while she was waiting for Wings to finish drying. Otherwise she'd just have to do it later.

Bandit frisked after her as she pushed the wheelbarrow out of the barn and across the yard to the gate.

"Stay back," Haley told the dog as she reached for the latch. "I'm serious, Bandit. Is your memory that short?"

She grimaced, trying not to flash back to the day last fall when Bandit had darted out through the gate and into the country highway beyond, where he'd been hit by a car. Haley still blamed herself for the accident—she hadn't been paying attention and had left the gate ajar.

But seriously, you'd think he wouldn't be so excited to get out here anymore after what happened, she thought as she shoved the dog back with her foot.

"Sit. Stay," she told him sternly.

Bandit stared at her. His lean hindquarters sank halfway to the ground, but as soon as Haley reached for the latch again, he leaped to his feet, trying to push past her to the gate.

"Bandit, no!" she exclaimed in frustration. "Stay! Sit! Aargh!"

She abandoned the wheelbarrow and hurried back into the barn, where she grabbed a handful of kibble out of the can in the feed room. Bandit shadowed her the whole time, drooling slightly when he spotted the kibble. One of the other dogs, a chubby beagle mix, spied the treats too and got up from his nap on a pile of saddle blankets. He yawned and waddled after Haley as she hurried back out of the barn.

"Okay," Haley said when they were in the barnyard again. "Bandit, it's time to do some serious training. For real this time."

After the accident, Haley had spent some time working on the dog's training, figuring that if he had a better grasp of basic commands, it would be easier to keep him safe. But his cast had gotten in the way at first, and later it had been too snowy and cold to spend any more time outside than necessary, and then she'd just plain forgotten about it.

But now it was time to get back to that training. Past time, really. Especially since Bandit still seemed ready to race out into the road any chance he got. Haley wasn't going to let that happen again on her watch. No way.

"Let's start with an easy one." Haley held up a piece of kibble. "Bandit, sit!"

Bandit barked excitedly, leaping up and trying to grab

the kibble out of Haley's hand. Meanwhile the beagle mix circled her, almost tripping Haley when she stepped back to avoid Bandit's lunge.

"No, no!" Haley cried. "Bandit, quit it! And, you—out of the way."

She pocketed the kibble, grabbed Bandit by the collar, and nudged the other dog away with her foot. Bandit wagged his tail and let his tongue loll out happily.

"Sit, boy." Keeping hold of his collar with one hand, Haley used the other to press down on the dog's bony rump. "Sit!"

Bandit blinked at her, then finally sat. Haley smiled.

"Good boy!" she exclaimed, pulling out a piece of kibble and tossing it to him.

The beagle mix whined, looking pathetic, so Haley tossed him a piece too. Then she returned her attention to Bandit.

"Okay, now stay." She held up her hand, palm out toward the dog. That was the way her uncle trained all the dogs on the farm when he had time, and Haley knew that Bandit had learned the basics when he'd first arrived. "Stay, Bandit!"

At his name, Bandit leaped to his feet and barked. Then he trotted over and sat down on Haley's foot.

Apparently sensing that he might be missing more treats, the beagle mix raced over to Bandit. Bandit jumped to his feet again, bowed to the other dog, and then raced around in circles.

"Bandit, no!" Haley cried, pounding her fist on her thigh in frustration. "Get back here, you idiot!"

"Having problems, Haley?"

Spinning around, Haley saw her cousin Danny standing by the backyard gate and grinning at her. Right behind him was Owen Lemke.

Haley's face went hot. What was Owen doing here? And why did he have to appear just when she was yelling at her dog and sounding like a crazy person?

"How's it going, Haley?" Owen stepped into the barnyard and stuck his hands into the pockets of his jeans. "What're you doing?"

"Nothing," Haley blurted out. "I mean, I was just— What are you doing here?" She glared at him.

"Wow, testy much?" Danny said with a snort. "He's here because we're going for a ride."

"What?" Haley shifted her glare to her cousin.

"Turkey season starts soon, remember?" Danny shrugged. "We're going to ride out and scope out the best spots to put our blinds."

Haley blinked, belatedly recalling that Owen had gone hunting with Danny on their property a few times the previous year. The two boys were only a year apart in school and hung out sometimes, especially when they wanted to go fishing or hunting. "Oh," she said. "Uh, okay."

"Glad we have your permission." Owen grinned. "By the way, how was that sissy English show thingy of yours? You and the runt win a fancy blue ribbon, or what?"

"No," Haley said bluntly. "Speaking of horses, where's Chance? I thought you said you're going riding."

"Pop said he could ride Chico," Danny replied, waving a hand toward the pasture where the family's three quarter horses were grazing.

"Good, he's about Owen's speed," Haley snapped. "Nice and slow and boring."

"Ooookay." Owen traded a look with Danny. "Whatever, Haley. See you later."

Bandit dashed after the boys as they headed into the barn. Haley took advantage of his departure to shove the wheelbarrow out through the gate, and dumped it with a little more force than absolutely necessary.

Stupid boys, she thought. *Why can't they ever take anything seriously?*

By the time she returned, the boys had gone off to the pasture to fetch their horses. Haley hurried to Wings's stall, and was relieved to find that he was finally dry beneath his cooler. She yanked it off and hung it on the stall door, then went to turn him out.

On her way to the pasture, the boys passed her, leading Chico and Jet, but they just nodded and continued their conversation. Haley and Wings continued to the pasture, where Rusty was standing forlornly at the gate calling for his herd mates. He stretched his head over the fence when Wings approached, seeming relieved.

"Okay, go on in, boy." Haley patted the pony on the rump as he stepped through the gate. "And rest up—we have that lesson tomorrow, remember?"

That made her feel a little more cheerful. Jan was great at helping her students pinpoint problems and then solve them. She'd be able to help Haley and Wings regain their mojo, if anyone could. Jan would help make sure that next time Haley and Wings really would come home with that fancy blue ribbon.

◆ CHAPTER ◆

7

SUNDAY WAS WARM AND STILL, WITH A HINT of the pleasant spring weather that would be arriving before long. Haley leaned forward in the passenger seat of her uncle's truck as he pulled up to Jan's modest clapboard barn, set in the midst of stubbly winter fields that would soon be sprouting with corn and hay and soybeans. Andrew was already grooming his horse in the outdoor wash rack between the barn and the outdoor ring.

By the time Haley had unloaded Wings and led him over to the tie ring beside Turbo, Kyle and Augie had arrived too. Andrew had Turbo tacked up before the others, but he stood nearby and let the thoroughbred graze on the wispy bits of early spring grass while Haley and Kyle finished getting their horses ready.

"So," Kyle said. "I talked to my parents, and I'm going to do that event next weekend too."

"Cool." Haley looked up from trying to brush a manure stain out of the white part of her pony's coat. It was still too cold for a proper bath, so keeping him clean was a constant challenge. "Guess we'll all be fighting for that blue ribbon again."

Andrew laughed, but Kyle shook his head. "Nope, I'll leave that to you two. I'm going to drop back a level."

"Really?" That made Haley look up again. At unrecognized events it was common for there to be levels well below beginner novice, which was the lowest recognized level. She and Wings had done their first competition at something called mini-amoeba level, over a cross-country course that had been totally enclosed in a large fenced field, with obstacles ranging from small logs on the ground to railroad ties and simple flower boxes.

Jan appeared at the end of the barn aisle just in time to hear Kyle's comment. She was leading a tall, elegant dapple-gray gelding. The horse was fully tacked up in Jan's jumping saddle, with a running martingale attached to his bridle. Haley had met Cancun the last time she'd come to Jan's for a lesson. He was a talented jumper but had turned out to be a little too lively and bold for his previous career as a show hunter. His new owner wanted to event him, so Jan was teaching him the basics.

"I got your text about dropping back a level, Kyle," Jan said. "I think it's a good idea. You guys did fine last time, but I think you'd both gain confidence from a good stadium round, and dropping down is probably the best way to do it." She glanced at Wings. "Haley, you might want to consider trying elementary this time too. You and Wings could probably—"

"No!" Haley blurted out. "I mean, I don't think that's necessary. We'll be ready for BN this time."

Jan raised her eyebrows. "Okay," she said with a shrug. "Thought that stop might've shaken you up a little—you were awfully quiet afterward."

"I was just trying to figure out what I'd done wrong so I could fix it." Haley squared her shoulders, looking her trainer in the eye. "And I know we can do this."

Jan nodded. "Fine. Sounds like you're confident, so no worries."

Kyle was watching Cancun as the big gray horse sniffed noses with Turbo. "Are you riding with us today?" he asked the trainer.

"Thought I would, if nobody minds." Jan tugged lightly on the reins to pull her horse away from the other gelding. "We probably won't jump, but Cancun could use some more experience just being in the ring with other horses before we tackle the warm-up area next weekend."

"You mean you're entering him in the event?" Kyle asked. "The one we're all doing?"

"Uh-huh. We're going to give BN a whirl, see how he does."

Haley was still a little distracted by Jan's suggestion, however mild, that she and Wings drop down a level. But now she tuned in again. "You'll be competing against us?" she blurted out.

Jan chuckled. "Looks that way. But don't worry. Cancun and I won't be chasing ribbons. This is his first event—we're just going to give it a go, try to have a nice, calm dressage test and then see how he reacts to being out on a cross-country course in an unfamiliar place." She patted the gray gelding. "I know he won't have any trouble with the physical part—he's jumped much bigger than BN height before—but the mental part? That's an open question."

Haley nodded, though she knew that Jan wouldn't enter the event if she wasn't pretty confident that the horse was ready. Haley tried not to think about that as she grabbed her saddle.

Suddenly Jan's phone buzzed. Pulling it out of her pocket, she glanced at the screen. "I've got to take this," she said. "See you all in the ring in five?"

"We'll be there," Kyle told her.

Haley watched the trainer hurry away with her phone pressed to her ear and Cancun trailing along behind her. "Wow," Haley said. "It's weird to think about competing against Jan, right?"

"Yeah." Andrew shrugged. "That sort of thing happens a lot in eventing, though."

"I guess." Haley knew he was right. Upper-level riders often rode young or green horses at the lower levels as part of their training. At the bigger recognized events down toward Chicago, where Haley had spectated a few times, it wasn't unusual to see former Olympians riding at training level—and not always winning either.

"Makes me even happier that I'm dropping back," Kyle joked. "So I guess you guys had better school extra hard this week, huh?"

"Don't worry. Already on it." Haley set the saddle onto her pony's back. "Wings and I have been working really hard all week, especially on dressage. I'm starting to see dressage letters whenever I close my eyes to go to sleep."

Andrew chuckled. "I'm not quite that bad. Turbo gets burned out on dressage pretty easily, so we've mostly been hacking out. It's easier to work on stuff like bending and adjusting our stride if he doesn't know it's dressage, you know?" He winked and gave his horse a pat.

"Wow." Kyle shook his head and grinned. "Guess I'm just a slacker compared to you two. Augie and I took the week off from schooling, pretty much. Just went on the trails a couple of times, and did some barrel racing with my neighbor on Friday afternoon." He shrugged. "Well, folding-chair racing, technically. We didn't have any barrels."

Andrew laughed as he handed Kyle the bridle hanging near Augie's head. "Sounds fun. Come on, let's get out there."

Jan was already in the ring when they arrived. She was in the saddle, walking Cancun on a loose rein while talking on the phone. When she saw the students coming, she hung up and stuck the phone back into her pocket.

"Let's get them warmed up with some basic flatwork," she called. "Loose rein, ride off your seats and legs, and let's play follow the leader."

She led the way through their warm-up, starting off on the rail and then switching to circles and figure eights around the jumps set up in the ring. Wings felt lively and alert, pricking his ears at each jump as they passed it.

"I know, buddy," Haley whispered, giving him a quick rub on the withers as they followed Turbo around another turn. "I can't wait to start jumping either."

When all the horses were loose and listening, Jan halted her horse in the center of the ring. She pointed to a line of two jumps—a vertical to a panel.

"We'll start here," she said. "Treat it as a gymnastic—trot in, canter out. Haley, you're up first."

Haley nodded, turning Wings away from the others to begin her approach to the line Jan had indicated. The jumps were small, maybe two foot three or so. Wings tried to break into a canter as soon as he realized they were heading for a jump, but Haley held him back.

"Trot, boy," she said firmly. "Trrrrot."

She could feel his energy building beneath her as he surged toward the vertical. He leaped over it and landed at a forward canter, kicking up his heels after the first stride.

Haley laughed. "Focus, Wingsie!" she cried as the pony charged ahead, ears pricked. "There's another jump coming."

The pony leaped over the second fence easily, and Haley had to circle him several times before he broke back to a choppy trot and then a walk.

Jan was smiling as Haley and Wings returned to the

group. "Well, he certainly seems enthusiastic today," she quipped. "Andrew? You're next."

Turbo completed the simple exercise easily, and then it was Kyle's turn. He had no trouble keeping his horse at a trot; in fact, a few strides out Jan called, "Leg! Keep him moving forward!"

Kyle glanced over at her, then kicked, but Augie barely responded. The buckskin gelding lurched over the first jump, barely lifting his feet, and the top rail clanked to the ground.

"Keep going!" Jan called.

Kyle nodded, kicking harder. Augie finally lumbered into a canter, and the next jump went much better.

Jan had already dismounted and was leading Cancun over to reset the first fence. "Okay, let's try that again, Kyle," she said. "Start at a canter this time. I think we need to make sure Mr. Augie's awake before we move on."

Andrew and Kyle chuckled, but Haley's smile felt forced and she opened and closed her hands on the reins impatiently. It had been a while since she'd shared a stadium jumping lesson with Kyle—long enough to have almost forgotten what it was like. Augie was super-reliable over just about any kind of cross-country fence, since the horse knew they were solid and wouldn't give way if he hit them. But he was smart enough to recognize that the jumps in the ring fell down much more easily, and he tended to get lazy about picking up his feet. That was why he had so much trouble in that phase.

And sure enough, as the lesson progressed, Augie stayed true to form. He was a little better over the panel and gate, but any top rail was more likely than not to end up on the ground.

"Sorry," Kyle said breathlessly, pulling his horse to a halt after making mincemeat out of yet another line of fences. "We haven't really done any jumping since the event. Guess it shows, huh?"

"It's all right." Jan slid down from the saddle again. "Let me put the fences down a couple of holes, and let's see if it goes any better then."

Haley swallowed back a sigh of frustration. She'd hoped that today's lesson would really help her and Wings, get them both sharp for next week's competition. But here they were spending their time on remedial stuff instead!

I might as well have stayed home and schooled on my own, she thought.

But she almost immediately shook her head. She always learned a lot in Jan's lessons, no matter what the students did. This would be good for her and Wings. At the very least it was a reminder of what *not* to do.

Finally, at the end Jan set up a full course at BN show height. She sent Andrew and Turbo out over it first, and then Haley and Wings.

By the time Wings had landed after the final fence, Haley was smiling again. He'd felt great out there, attacking every jump with gusto and not even coming close to touching a rail.

"Great!" Jan called. "Wings is such a super little jumper—I swear he has more scope than most horses two hands taller than him!"

"Thanks." Haley dropped her reins and leaned down to give Wings a big hug around the neck. "See? Told you we were ready for BN." She grinned at Jan to show that she was just kidding. Well, mostly, anyway.

Jan laughed. "Okay, okay. Now if you all don't mind, I'd like to see if Cancun and I are ready for BN. If you're in a hurry, you can go cool down outside; otherwise stay in the middle, okay?"

"Sure!" Haley quickly gathered her reins and nudged Wings into a walk, riding him toward the open area at the center of the ring. She was glad that Jan had decided to jump Cancun today after all. Haley loved watching her trainer ride, and especially loved watching her jump. The two boys joined her, letting their horses stand on a loose rein while Jan trotted and cantered around the ring a couple of times to get Cancun loosened up again. Then Jan aimed the big dapple gray at the first fence of the course.

Cancun's ears pricked sharply forward when he realized they were heading for the jump. His canter slowed, and he drifted sideways—first to the left, and then when Jan stopped him, to the right. But Jan kept his head pointed toward the fence the whole time, and when they got there, he hesitated only slightly before leaping over it and racing forward on the far side.

Haley held her breath. She could hear Jan talking to

the big gelding, though the trainer's aids were so subtle that it didn't look like she was doing anything else. Haley knew she was, though, since Cancun tipped an ear back toward his rider, and his pace slowed and collected. He met the second fence neatly out of stride, though he jumped a little higher than necessary and swished his tail upon landing.

Next came a vertical that Jan had decorated with brightly colored fake flowers to help prepare the horses for whatever type of filler they might find on the jumps at an event. Cancun slowed down again as he approached, his head going up as he gave the flowers a hard stare.

But once again Jan kept him moving forward, and once again Cancun hesitated only for a split second before leaping over the jump. He spurted forward on the far side and let out a small buck, which Jan sat through easily before sending him on.

"Hey, look, Wings—you're not the only one who does that," Kyle commented with a grin.

Haley laughed and patted her pony. "But he looks cuter doing it," she told the boys.

Then she watched as Jan circled Cancun back around, aiming him at the flower fence again. Doing that at a real event would get you eliminated, but Haley knew it wasn't about doing things the proper way right now. Jan was schooling Cancun, making sure he was learning all the time, and this was what Jan thought he needed to do to learn what she was teaching him. And it seemed to work, since the gray gelding cleared the flowers nicely the second time.

After that Jan continued on to the next jump, not deviating again until they'd finished the course. "Wow, that was nice," Andrew commented. "But it's pretty obvious why Cancun flunked out of hunters."

Haley chuckled and nodded. She'd ridden show hunters for a year or so before discovering eventing, and she knew that those horses had to look calm and easy to ride, neither of which was true of the big gray gelding. But it was just as obvious that Cancun had scope to spare for the small fences he'd just jumped.

"I wonder why she's starting at BN instead of novice or even training," Haley said, her eyes never leaving the trainer as Cancun cantered around the far turn before coming back to a smooth, collected trot.

Kyle shrugged. "Like she said, she doesn't want to overwhelm him," he said. "It'll be easier to help him get used to the commotion if she doesn't have to worry about him actually, you know, getting over the jumps."

"Yeah, I guess." Haley bit her lip. "Anyway, I bet they're going to win our division."

"Probably," Kyle agreed, and Andrew nodded.

But that doesn't mean Wings and I can't try to beat her, Haley thought. *And even if we don't, there's no shame coming in second to someone like Jan. That'll be just as good as winning, right?*

"Toss me that hoofpick?" Kyle called.

Haley grabbed the pick she'd just used to clean out Wings's feet after the lesson. Ducking under her pony's neck, she handed it to Kyle, who was in the next set of ties in the wash rack.

"Thanks," Kyle said. "So anyway, I hope you guys'll still talk to me at the event even though I'll be a lowly tadpole-level rider."

Andrew laughed. "We'll see," he teased.

"What about you, Haley?" Kyle turned to grin at her.

"Of course." She rolled her eyes, then returned to rubbing the sweat marks off her pony's girth area. "So do you think the lower jumps will help Augie, like Jan said?"

"Hope so." Kyle leaned over, grabbed one of Augie's hooves, and ran the pick around the frog. "But I'm sure it's mostly my fault he's so lazy in stadium. So I'm actually hoping it helps me."

"It will," Andrew told him. He smiled and patted his horse, who was on the other side of Augie. "I'm hoping Turbo and I have another good day and maybe improve our dressage score a little. Jan thinks we might be able to move up to novice by the end of the summer if we keep on the way we've been doing."

"Really?" Haley felt a pang of unease as she flashed back to Jan's suggestion earlier about her moving down a level. "Um, Wings and I have already competed at novice, so I'm sure we'll be back there soon. You know, after we get over whatever happened last time. Which I'm thinking was probably a farrier thing, by the way."

"Really?" Kyle looked up from his horse's hoof. "What kind of thing?"

"I don't know yet—the farrier's coming on Tuesday. But there was obviously some reason Wings stopped at that jump." Haley laughed self-consciously. "You know, other than my distracted riding, I mean. He's gone ahead and jumped lots of times when I wasn't paying attention. That's half the reason I fell off so much when we first started eventing."

Both boys laughed, though they looked a little confused. "Okay," Kyle said. "Anyway, you guys might not want to rush getting to novice, or you'll have to compete against that Riley girl and her fancy schmancy horse."

"True," Andrew agreed with a smile.

"No way. I can't wait to face her again," Haley said. "When we're on our game, Wings the super pony can totally beat Riley and her horse any day of the week." She stared at the boys as if daring them to argue. "You'll see."

◆ CHAPTER ◆
8

"IS IT FRIDAY YET?" TRACEY ASKED WITH A groan.

Haley took the seat beside her friend and dropped her schoolbag at her feet. "Nope. Only Tuesday," she said. "Good thing too, because Wings and I still have a ton to do before our event on Saturday."

"Good thing for you, maybe, but I'm already brain-dead after that test we just had in science." Tracey opened her purse and dug out a lip gloss. "Talk about brutal!"

"I know, right?" Emma was sitting behind Haley. She leaned forward, her pale hair falling over her forehead as she stared through her glasses at their English teacher, who had just come into the room. "And now it looks like we're getting our English tests back."

Haley felt a quiver of anxiety as she watched Ms. Reyes grab a stack of papers from her desk. They'd had an essay test the previous Friday, and Haley had been so busy with Wings all that week that she hadn't quite finished the reading.

Ms. Reyes started calling each student to the front of the room to get his or her test. When it was Haley's turn, the teacher looked worried.

"Oh, Haley," she said with a sigh. "I know you can do better than this."

Haley winced as the teacher handed her a paper with a big red C-minus scrawled at the top. "Um, sorry," she said. "I'll do better next time."

"I hope so." Ms. Reyes shook her head. "In the meantime I'd like you to have your aunt or uncle sign this and bring it back."

"What?" Haley blurted out, alarmed now. Aunt Veronica and Uncle Mike took school very seriously. If she showed them this grade, they might make her skip the event on Saturday! And she couldn't let that happen. She had to prove that she and Wings had what it took to win—and the sooner the better.

"Yes, but you can tell them you still have a chance to bring the grade up." Ms. Reyes grabbed another sheet of paper out of a drawer. "Here's an extra credit worksheet. Write at least three paragraphs for each question and turn it in on Monday, and if you do a good job, I should be able to bump that test score up at least one full grade, if not more."

"Oh. Um . . ." Haley took the paper, mentally calculating how long it would take her to complete the extra credit work. Once Saturday's event was over, she could probably spend most of Sunday on homework. That should be long enough. "Okay, thanks. I will."

She slunk back to her seat. "Well?" Emma said, holding up her own B-plus test. "How'd you do?"

Haley showed her and Tracey the test paper. "Ouch," Tracey said, glancing at the C-plus on her own sheet. "You did even worse than me."

"I know." Haley stared at the ugly red letter. "I just

hope my aunt and uncle don't make me back out of my event on Saturday."

Emma's eyes widened. "Do you think they might? But Tracey and I were going to come cheer you on and everything!"

"Yeah." Tracey shrugged and tugged on her bangs. "We still feel guilty for missing the last one."

"It's okay." Haley had been disappointed about that, but given what had happened, things had turned out for the best. It had been embarrassing enough being eliminated in front of her fellow riders, without having to explain the rules of eventing—again—to her non-horsey best friends as well. "But yeah, I'll let you know what happens."

She tucked the test and the extra credit sheet into her bag, trying not to worry about it. She'd talk her aunt and uncle into letting her compete this weekend, no matter what it took. She had to. Her pride as a rider was at stake.

That evening Haley helped her aunt load the dinner dishes into the dishwasher even though technically it was Danny's turn. Once that was finished and her uncle was halfway through his second cup of decaf, she finally pulled out the test paper.

"Um, Ms. Reyes wanted you guys to sign this," she said, handing it to her uncle.

Aunt Veronica hurried over to glance at the paper over his shoulder. "Oh, Haley," she said, her voice sharp with disappointment.

"I know, I know," Haley said quickly. "But don't worry. Ms. Reyes said I can bring up the grade with extra credit work. See?" She showed them the sheet.

Her aunt examined it. "Well, good," she said. "But you shouldn't need extra credit to keep your grades up, Haley."

"Right." Uncle Mike gazed at Haley, stroking his mustache thoughtfully. "Your aunt and I have noticed you've been working extra hard with Wings lately. I hope you're not letting that affect your studies."

"I'm not." Haley gulped, telling herself it wasn't exactly a lie. Okay, so she'd been letting a few things slide lately, school-wise. For instance, she hadn't even started tonight's homework yet, since she'd spent all afternoon waiting for the farrier, who'd been running late. She was sure she could make up for all of it after the event, though. "I mean I won't. Don't worry."

Her aunt and uncle traded a long look. "Haley," Aunt Veronica said, sitting down and patting the chair beside her. "We know you take your eventing very seriously, and we've always supported that."

Haley sank into the chair and nodded wordlessly. It was true—her aunt and uncle were both horse people themselves, and they'd always done whatever they could to help Haley improve her riding, from gifting her with lessons for all her birthdays and Christmases when she'd been younger, to letting Wings come live at their place when the neighbors had offered Haley that free lease. Aunt Veronica was always willing to meet the vet or farrier when their appointments fell during the school day, and Uncle Mike had hauled Haley and Wings to more lessons, shows, and events than she could count. She'd never be able to thank them enough for all they'd given her.

"I know," she said. "Thanks."

"You're welcome. But at your age, school is your most important job," Uncle Mike said gravely.

"That's right," his wife agreed. "We know you can do the work, Haley. You just need to make it a priority."

"I do," Haley blurted out, afraid of what might be coming next. She couldn't help flashing back to the time when they'd made Jake quit the baseball team after he'd flunked a school project. "I swear. I—I just had a bad day, that's all. It won't happen again. Please, just give me a chance to prove that, okay? I'll show you guys I can handle school *and* riding."

Her aunt and uncle traded another long look. "Weeeeell . . . ," Aunt Veronica said, drawing the word out so long that Haley could hardly stand it. "When is your extra credit work due?"

"Monday," Haley said.

"All right. Then we'd like for you to have it finished by Friday," Aunt Veronica said. "*Before* you go to that event."

"But—" Haley began, her mind already racing with everything she had to do to get ready—not to mention her regular homework and chores.

"But nothing." Uncle Mike's voice was firm. "You heard your aunt. Do you really want to argue?"

"No, sorry," Haley said meekly. "Um, thanks. I'd better go get started on it now."

When her aunt and uncle dismissed her, Haley dashed upstairs. Flopping onto her bed, she grabbed her laptop and logged on to the Pony Post, practically shaking with relief. She'd filled the other girls in on the test situation right after school, and Brooke and Nina had already left notes of concern, though Haley barely skimmed them now before opening a new text box.

> [HALEY] Guess what? The event is still on! All I
> have to do is, you know, not sleep between now
> and then so I can get everything done . . . but hey,
> been there done that, lol!

◆ ◆ ◆

Haley glanced up from her English book as Wings snorted and hung his head out over his stall door, a wispy bit of hay hanging from his lips. She was sitting in the middle of the barn aisle on an upturned bucket with her homework spread out around her.

"Don't be impatient. You can go out as soon as you're dry," Haley told him.

It was Wednesday afternoon, and they'd just finished their dressage schooling session. It had been a short one, partly because Wings had done really well, rounding up almost immediately and dancing effortlessly through the movements, and partly because Haley had too much to do to spend more time in the saddle.

At the sound of her voice, Bandit jumped to his feet. He'd been snoozing on her math book, but now he barked, wagged his tail, and did a *Let's play* bow.

"Sorry, no time to play right now." Suddenly remembering that she hadn't worked on the dog's training since getting interrupted the previous Saturday, Haley cleared her throat. "Sit, Bandit! Sit!"

She pointed at the dog. He stared at her and barked again, then sat for about a tenth of a second before leaping up again and racing around in a circle, scattering papers everywhere.

"Bandit, no!" Haley cried, grabbing for her schoolbook before it landed in a stray pile of manure she hadn't picked up yet. "Bad dog!"

He ignored her, sniffing noses with Wings, who was stretching his head out to see what was going on. Haley strode over and grabbed Bandit by the collar.

"I said sit," she said firmly, pushing his haunches to the ground. "Sit!"

Bandit obeyed this time, gazing up at her with his soft brown eyes. Haley smiled.

"Good dog. Now stay." She let go of his collar and stepped back. He popped to his feet and took a step toward her. "No!" she scolded. "Sit, stay!"

She put him back in the sit. It took a few tries and an increasingly stern tone, but finally she convinced him to stay for a few seconds.

"Okay, that's better. Good boy." She looked around for a ball or stick to toss for the dog, figuring he deserved a reward. But by the time she had found a ragged tennis ball in the tack room, Bandit had disappeared.

Haley shrugged. Oh well. It was for the best. She really didn't have time to play with him anyway. Not if she wanted to get everything done so she could go win that event.

Picking up her English book, she settled onto the bucket and got back to work.

Haley couldn't stop yawning as she crawled into bed that night. Still, she couldn't resist checking in with the Pony Post before she went to sleep. She'd filled them in earlier not only on what her aunt and uncle had said, but also on the changes she was making to her training plans so she could still fit everything in and be prepared enough to win.

She smiled when she saw that all three of her friends had left messages in response to hers.

[NINA] Glad u can still do the event, H. But I hope u can relax a little after u finish the extra credit stuff. Don't forget how crazy u got b4 that clinic, right?

[BROOKE] Ya, Nina has a point, Haley. It's just 1 event. U will have another one soon, so don't make yourself sick over it or anything.

[MADDIE] Don't wanna pile on, but the girls are right. Chill, Hales! U and the Wingster are super-fit and ready; u don't need to worry about it! Get ur school stuff done and then you can forget about it and have fun on Sat!!

Haley frowned as she read over the posts again, which definitely weren't the type of thing she'd been expecting to find when she'd logged on. What were her friends so worked up about? This wasn't like back in the fall, when she'd been so desperate to earn enough money for that clinic that she really had pushed herself a little too hard. This wasn't the same thing at all.

I thought at least Maddie would understand, Haley thought. *She's an athlete too—she's played soccer for as long as I've been riding, and she almost joined that traveling team, even.*

She blinked, one word echoing in her head—"almost."

Maybe Maddie couldn't understand either. When she'd been offered the chance to try out for a prestigious traveling soccer team, she'd ended up turning it down, not wanting to take time away from other activities including riding. Haley could appreciate that, but still, she wondered if it meant Maddie didn't have the same kind of killer edge Haley did, the determination and focus it took to win.

"Whatever," she muttered, closing the computer without bothering to respond to the posts.

Crawling into bed, she pushed her friends' comments out of her mind. Instead she reviewed her dressage test in her head until she fell asleep.

◆ CHAPTER ◆
9

I DID IT, HALEY THOUGHT AS SHE BEGAN her cross-country course walk on Saturday. She glanced past Jan, Andrew, and Kyle, who were discussing the first jump, to take in the people dotting the course and the horse trailers, barns, and fluttering flags beyond. *Somehow I did it. I can hardly believe I'm really here!*

The previous three days had been busy, busy, busy. Haley had spent every waking moment either in the saddle or at her desk—well, except when she'd been doing chores or in school or cleaning her tack or the zillion other things she'd managed to squeeze in.

But it had all been worth it. Because here she was, about to show the world—or at least this little corner of Wisconsin—what she and her pony could really do.

That weekend's event was at a farm where Haley and Wings had competed before, though it had been a couple of years. It wasn't as fancy as the site of the previous event, but the footing was usually decent, and the owners always brought in good judges, so the events were very popular.

"Check it out," Haley told Jan as they hiked up a slight hill after the first jump. "Looks like they redid the water complex."

Jan squinted off to the left at the small, square man-made pond, which had sandy footing leading down into one long side and several jumps arrayed around the other edges. "Yeah," she said. "I've heard that the footing is much more consistent now and it rides pretty well."

"Good." Kyle zipped his Windbreaker up a little higher. "Because it's a little chilly today for a swim."

Haley laughed, pushing back a strand of hair that the wind had just whipped across her forehead. It was one of those early spring days when the sun shone so fiercely that it could make you think it was actually warm out, and yet a trace of winter's chill enveloped you every time you got caught in the gusty breeze. That kind of weather tended to get Wings—and a lot of other horses—a little riled up and snorty. She would have to be extra careful to keep him calm and focused in dressage and stadium, but the extra energy would only help them out here on cross-country.

"Look," Andrew murmured, breaking into her thoughts. "There's Riley."

Haley followed his gaze. The older girl was just ahead of them, frowning with concentration as she paced off the approach to a small log a few strides after the water.

"Hey," Haley said when she noticed the color of the flag on the log jump. "I wonder if Riley knows she's looking at the BN log there. I thought she was doing novice this time."

Andrew shook his head. "I talked to her when I first got here," he said. "She decided to stay at BN one more time after all. She wants to move up at a recognized event—says it'll mean more that way, or something."

"Oh." Haley bit her lip, a little dismayed. She hadn't taken Riley into account when she'd been prepping for today. Athena had looked awfully good in dressage last time; if Riley fixed her steering issues, they'd be hard to beat.

But then Haley shrugged. Hard, yes. Impossible? No way. She and Wings could do anything. And beating Riley and her fancy horse would make today's victory even sweeter.

After the course walk Haley and the others hurried back to check on the horses. Jan's trailer was parked at the edge of a flat field adjoining the cow pasture next door. Most of the horses, including Wings, were tied to the trailer where they'd left them. But Jan's assistant was there hand-grazing Cancun, who kept lifting his head every few seconds to stare around with wide, nervous eyes.

"How's he doing?" Jan asked, taking the big dapple-gray horse's lead from the younger woman.

The assistant shrugged. "Still kinda amped. But hey, that'll make your dressage even more interesting, right?"

Jan chuckled, giving Cancun a pat. "For sure."

Just then a cow in the neighboring pasture mooed, and the big gray leaped in place, spinning around and snorting. For a second Haley thought he might rip the lead out of Jan's hand and take off.

"Easy, boy," the trainer said, giving a sharp tug on the line to get the horse's attention back on her. "Don't go all mental on me, okay? Those aren't horse-eating cows, I promise. Look at Wings. He's not paying any attention to them at all, and he's, like, half your size!"

Haley smiled. "He'd better not be afraid of cows," she joked. "Otherwise we wouldn't have much fun at team penning."

Her smile faded slightly when she thought back to that last penning. She was pretty sure now that it had to have been the culprit in their poor performance last time out, since the farrier hadn't found anything wrong with Wings's feet that could explain their jumping problems.

Well, this time we shouldn't have to worry, since we've been totally focused on eventing, Haley thought. *No team penning, no distractions.*

As Haley went to check Wings's hay net, she noticed a large, shiny three-horse trailer pulling carefully past over the rutted ground. She immediately recognized the girl in the passenger seat.

"Look," she told Kyle, who was passing by with more hay for Augie's net. "I guess that girl Claire's doing this one too."

He looked and nodded. "Figures," he said. "She definitely wasn't happy with her placing last time. Probably wants to redeem herself or something."

Claire's trailer pulled into a free spot just across the way. Haley watched as a well-dressed man hopped out of the driver's seat and hurried around to open the back. Claire got out too and stood watching as the man disappeared inside. He emerged a moment later leading a very tall dark bay gelding with a sculpted head and an elegantly arched neck.

"I wonder whose horse that is," Haley commented to Kyle. She waited for the man to go back in to get Bella, but instead he handed Claire the lead rope and closed the trailer door.

Meanwhile Claire spotted them and headed over, the big gelding trailing behind her. "Hi, you guys," she called out. "I didn't know you were coming to this event. That Riley girl told me about it at the last one."

"Us too." Haley was watching the horse, who was surveying his surroundings with interest but no sign of nerves. "Who's that?"

Claire glanced over her shoulder. "My new horse," she said. "His name's Dragon. Isn't he cute?"

"Cute" wasn't the word Haley would have chosen. Wings was cute. Augie was cute. Even Turbo and Cancun were cute in their own ways. Next to them Dragon looked like a lion among house cats. Good-looking and impressive, but maybe a little intimidating.

"He used to event at the upper levels down in Illinois," Claire went on without waiting for the others to respond. "Zina Charles even rode him once and said he was supertalented."

"Your new horse?" Haley echoed. She'd blinked at the mention of the rider who'd given that clinic in the fall, but she hadn't really moved on past Claire's first words. "But where's Bella? Isn't that her name—your nice bay mare?"

Claire's smug smile faded a little. "At my trainer's barn waiting to get sold," she snapped. "We just weren't getting along, and that last event proved it. My stupid ugly brown ribbon finally convinced Daddy to get me something better."

Kyle stared up at Dragon, looking awed. "Congratulations," he said. "He's—big."

"Almost seventeen hands." Claire's pleased smile returned. "He definitely won't have any trouble getting over those elementary jumps, right?"

"Elementary?" Haley echoed. "Aren't you doing BN again?"

"Nope." Claire reached up to stroke her horse's glossy neck. "Dragon and I are still getting to know each other, so my trainer suggested we drop back this time. But I'm sure we'll move up fast once we get used to each other."

The man strode over to them, cell phone in hand. "Your trainer just texted, Claire-bear," he said. "He wants you to meet him for your cross-country course walk pronto."

"Thanks, Daddy." Claire handed him Dragon's lead.

"See you guys later," she called over her shoulder as she hurried off in the direction of the cross-country course.

Haley watched Claire's father lead the big bay horse back over toward their trailer. She could hardly believe they'd bought a horse like Dragon for Claire to compete at elementary level. But whatever—at least Haley wouldn't have to worry about facing Dragon in her division. Let Kyle deal with competing against Claire's new, even fancier horse!

"Are you okay?" Haley brought Wings to a halt and looked back at Kyle. She'd just reached the gate of the warm-up ring, which was really only a large, mostly flat dirt paddock. At least a dozen horses and riders were already in there warming up for their dressage tests, and Haley and Kyle were about to join them. But Kyle had stopped his horse a few yards back and was fiddling with his reins.

He glanced at Haley, then shot a look over his shoulder in the direction of the parking area. "I think I should've waited for Jan," he said with a weak smile. "Augie feels kind of, I don't know, different or something?"

Haley glanced at the buckskin gelding, who looked as placid as ever. Then Augie lifted his head and pricked his ears as the distant sound of a moo drifted toward them on the wind.

She laughed. "He's okay. He's just missing his new friends the cows," she joked. She'd noticed that Augie, who had been tied closest to the cow pasture, had spent more time watching the spotted creatures than eating his hay. "Come on. You'll be fine."

"I don't know." Kyle glanced back again. "Jan will probably be here soon. Maybe I'll just get off and wait for her. You go ahead, though."

Haley swallowed a sigh, shooting a look toward the ring. Her dressage time was more than half an hour after Kyle's, so she had plenty of time before she had to do her real pre-test warm-up. However, she really wanted to get Wings out there now to loosen up, since he'd been standing around all morning so far—first during the long trailer ride here and then by Jan's trailer during the course walk. Besides, Kyle was right—Jan would be along soon. The trainer was just helping Andrew find a spare noseband in her tack box, since Turbo had managed to step on his bridle and break it.

Then Haley looked at Kyle's face, which was uncharacteristically anxious. "It's okay, I'm in no hurry," she told him. "Sure, he's a little distracted. But you know what to do. You just need to get his attention on you, right? Put him to work, make him focus."

"You sound like Jan." Kyle smiled at her, though it still looked a little forced.

"That's because she's told us that a million times," Haley said. "Come on. I'll ride with you out here for a minute before we tackle the warm-up ring, okay?"

She nudged Wings into a walk and rode him over to Augie. Kyle still looked anxious, but he started Augie walking too. They circled around the grassy area outside the warm-up for the next ten minutes. Every time Haley started to feel impatient, she reminded herself that lots of people had helped her through tough moments in the past—including Kyle himself when he'd run out and caught Wings after Haley had come off. That was one of the things she loved most about eventing. Riders were almost always ready to help someone, even the competition.

"Thanks for doing this, Haley," Kyle told her after a while, sounding a little more like his usual chipper self. He shot her a smile. "I don't know what I'd do if you weren't here. You're the best."

"It's cool." She smiled back and nodded toward the warm-up ring. "Ready to go in there yet?"

He hesitated. "Umm . . ."

Luckily, at that moment Haley spotted Jan and Andrew riding toward them from the direction of the parking area. Good. She just hoped she hadn't missed too much time out of her warm-up, because she was counting on a great dressage score to start their day off right.

Later Haley sat on Wings near the dressage ring, watching a young elementary rider do his test. Her turn was still quite a while away, but the elementary section was almost over, and she wanted to watch the first few beginner novice riders perform the test, to make sure she had it down cold.

Suddenly she heard voices calling her name. Twisting around in the saddle, she saw Tracey and Emma racing toward her. And they weren't alone. Two boys were trailing along behind them, looking a little out of place in their cowboy boots and Western belt buckles.

"Owen?" Haley blurted out as the little group reached her.

"Hey," Owen said, glancing out toward the ring. "So your friends talked Vance and me into coming to see what this fancy prancy English stuff is all about."

"Hi there, spotty pony," Vance said, stepping forward to pat Wings. "You look pretty snazzy all dressed up in your fancy clothes." He elbowed Owen. "Looks even less like a real horse than he did in a real saddle at the penning, huh?"

Owen laughed, but Haley frowned. She looked at Tracey and Emma, wondering why in the world they'd brought the two boys. No, scratch that—she knew why. Her friends were boy crazy, that was why.

"We didn't miss anything yet, did we, Hales?" Tracey asked, letting Wings sniff her hand like a dog. "Sorry we're a little late, but we decided to stop for sodas on the way."

"Heads up, coming through!" a rider on a stout gray horse hollered as he rode toward the gate.

Emma scooted aside quickly. "Oops," she said, sounding a little nervous. "Um, maybe we should go sit over there?" She gestured to a small set of bleachers along the long side of the ring, where spectators were watching the dressage riders perform.

"That's okay," Tracey said. "We're fine here."

"No, you should probably go sit down," Haley said. "You don't want to be in the way, right? And that way you'll be able to see my test in a little while."

"Sure, might as well sit," Owen said. "That'll make it less embarrassing when I fall asleep from boredom." He and Vance laughed loudly, moving off toward the bleachers.

"Doesn't he look hot in those jeans?" Tracey hissed at Haley, jerking her head after the boys.

Haley didn't know which boy she meant, and she didn't really care. For some reason seeing Owen here made her feel oddly jittery, and she definitely didn't need any distractions right now.

Fortunately, Tracey hurried after the others without waiting for a response. Haley took a few deep breaths and patted Wings, trying to forget about everything else except what she needed to do in a few minutes.

Kyle was one of the last people riding in the elementary division. By the time he entered the ring a couple of riders later, Haley had forgotten about her friends and the boys. Well, almost. Since Owen was here, she was actually starting to look forward to showing him just how versatile her Chincoteague pony really was.

Not only can we kick his behind in penning, but we can rock this event too! she thought, rubbing Wings's withers with a small smile.

She pushed that thought aside as Kyle began his test. He still looked a little nervous, but that was normal for him. Augie also looked normal—he seemed to have gotten over his fascination with the cows and was all business as he trotted up the center line.

The test went pretty well, with no major mistakes. A transition or two happened a little late, and some of the circles weren't exactly round, but Haley knew that Kyle had to be proud of himself and his horse. She cheered loudly as they left the ring.

"Thanks," Kyle said with a smile as he passed her. "But I was just the warm-up act. Here comes the main show."

Haley had no idea what he was talking about until she turned and saw Claire walking toward the gate atop her huge new horse. "Good luck, Claire!" Kyle called as she passed.

She didn't seem to hear him. Her expression was focused as she steered her horse through the gate. Haley watched with interest as Dragon swung into a big, ground-covering trot. His gaits seemed to be even fancier than those of Claire's previous horse. An audible murmur went up from the spectators when he trotted up the center line the first time, and watching his free walk, Haley finally understood what that movement was really supposed to look like.

Wow. He's really an amazing horse, she thought. *Probably too good for someone like Claire. . . .*

Feeling guilty for the uncharitable thought, she tried to forget about the rider and just enjoy watching the beautiful horse move. But she couldn't help noticing that even the amazing Dragon didn't automatically make his circles round on his own, and just like last time, Claire wasn't really bothering to ride all the way into the corners. But that just reminded Haley to do better herself.

When she reached the warm-up ring a short while later, only a few riders were in there. One of them was Andrew. He and Turbo were standing in the middle of the ring. The thoroughbred gelding's head was high, and he kept shaking it and trying to back up.

Haley rode over. "Everything okay?"

"Not really." Andrew shot her a frustrated frown. "Turbo must've been talking to Cancun or something, because one of those cows started mooing just as we were walking in here, and now he's all freaked out."

Haley was surprised. Turbo could be sensitive and overly energetic at times, and would occasionally spook at something unexpected, but he was usually pretty unflappable about strange sights and sounds. Jan said lots of ex-racehorses were like that, since they were exposed to so much at the track.

Then again, Haley supposed that most racetracks didn't have cows grazing in the infield. So maybe Turbo had finally found something that made him nervous.

She sneaked a peek at her watch, calculating how long she had before her ride time. If she wanted to win, she and Wings needed to be on top of their game. And while she was confident that Wings could jump any course after a short warm-up or none at all, she wasn't so sure when it came to dressage.

Turbo sidestepped, shaking his head so vigorously that Andrew could barely hold on to the reins. Haley quickly moved her pony around so he was between Turbo and the cow field.

"Okay, let's try this," she said. "I'll stay over here, and we'll walk around and show him it's no biggie."

"Thanks, Haley." Andrew shot her a grateful smile. "I'm sure he'll get over it in a second."

But it took a lot longer than a second before Turbo relaxed enough for Haley to begin her warm-up. She ended up rushing through it and had to hurry to get back into the ring in time.

"There you are!" Jan exclaimed when Haley arrived. "I was about to send out a search party."

"Sorry." Haley didn't bother to explain. The previous rider was already leaving, and by the time Haley and Wings got into the ring and halfway around the outside of the chains, the judge was ringing the bell.

Haley turned her pony and headed back down the side, feeling frazzled. She took a deep breath, trying to focus as she and Wings turned and entered at *A* for their test.

◆ CHAPTER ◆
10

FOR THE NEXT FEW MINUTES HALEY ALMOST felt as if she were watching her own dressage test from above rather than riding it. The first several movements were rushed and a little wobbly, and she felt anxiety rise inside her.

Not again! a little voice in her head cried out.

Haley closed her eyes for a moment as they trotted down the long side. Taking a deep breath, she finally felt herself relax into the saddle. She could do this. Good warm-up or not, she wasn't going to mess things up again. Not this time.

After that the test improved. Haley was careful to ride deep into every corner and focus on making every turn and circle as round as it could be. By the time they halted and saluted, she was smiling.

"Nicely done," the judge called as Haley rode forward afterward. She was an older woman with short gray hair and a pleasant smile. "What kind of pony is he?"

"Chincoteague," Haley replied proudly.

The judge smiled. "Thought so. One of my favorite breeds—ever since I read *Misty of Chincoteague* as a girl."

Haley grinned. "Me too!"

When she rode out of the ring, Jan was waiting for her. "Great recovery," she said, patting Wings on the shoulder and then Haley on the leg. "I could see you were tense when you started, but you pulled it out."

"Yeah." Haley's smile faded a little as she thought back over those first few movements. If only she'd had more time in the warm-up ring, she was sure she could have done better. Now, once again, they'd have to make up ground in the jumping phases.

After sliding down from the saddle, she loosened Wings's girth and started walking him around to cool him off. She wanted to stay by the ring to cheer on

Andrew and Jan, who would both be going soon.

Kyle had already taken Augie back to the trailers and returned to watch the others. He wandered over to join Haley as she walked. "You missed Riley's test while you were warming up," he said.

"Oh?" Haley tried to sound disinterested, though she didn't really succeed. "Perfect, I assume?"

"I wouldn't say that." Kyle shrugged. "She had a little trouble with her canter departs this time, and her horse looked kind of tense all the way through."

"Hmm." Haley felt a twinge of hope, though she tried not to get too excited. Kyle was so nice—he was probably just trying to make Haley feel better about her own botched movements.

Just then Haley's friends rushed over. She had almost forgotten they were there.

"Haley, you looked fabulous!" Emma exclaimed, giving her a hug.

"Yeah," Tracey agreed. "Don't you think so, Owen?"

Owen didn't answer. "Hey," he said to Kyle, glancing down at his breeches. "Nice pants."

Vance snorted with laughter, but Kyle just shot the other boys a tight smile. "I'm Kyle," he said. "And you are?"

"We're Haley's friends," Tracey told him. "I'm Tracey. That's Emma and Vance. And Owen, of course."

Kyle glanced down at Owen's well-worn cowboy boots. "You ride?"

"Yeah. We both do." Owen hooked a thumb toward Vance. "Real riding, that is—Western."

"Cool." Kyle shrugged. "That's probably fun. You know, if you don't want to jump."

Owen narrowed his eyes. "Why would we want to jump when we could do something fun instead?"

"Boys, boys!" Tracey sang out with a laugh. "Let's not fight, okay?" She turned toward Haley and winked broadly.

Haley had no idea why her friend looked so amused. She just wanted to get away from the boys' silly squabble and focus on what she had to do next.

"Excuse me," she said. "I need to take Wings back to the trailer now so he can rest before cross-country. Catch you guys later."

She took off without waiting for an answer.

"Come on." Kyle hurried over to Haley. She was brushing out Wings's tail, which had gotten a little tangled by the wind. "Jan's starting soon."

Haley nodded and dropped her tail brush. Jan had asked to go first in their division on cross-country so she could coach her students afterward. That meant they'd all be able to watch her ride, since none of their start times were coming up soon.

Most of the course was located in a pair of hilly adjoining fields below the parking area, with just a short portion going off through a patch of woods. That meant it was easy to see the majority of the jumps from the top of the rise near the corner of the cow pasture. Haley hurried out there and perched on the post-and-board fence between Andrew and Kyle. She could see her school friends standing with a small cluster of spectators below them on the hill, but she didn't call out to them. All four of them were shoving at one another and laughing, clearly not paying much attention to the action on the course. Haley wanted to focus on her trainer's ride, not the boys' goofy jokes.

"There she is." Andrew poked her in the arm, snapping her out of her thoughts.

Jan was riding toward the start box. "Cancun looks good," Kyle commented.

"Yeah." Haley watched the gray gelding lift his head and stare at the horse currently a few fences through the course. "Maybe still a little nervous, though."

"That's only natural. It's his first event, remember?" Andrew said.

Haley nodded and watched Cancun break into a jig as they neared the start box. She crossed her fingers, hoping Jan had a good ride.

A moment later Jan rode her horse into the start box and burst out a few seconds later. "And they're off!" Kyle cried like the announcer at a racetrack.

Haley smiled but didn't take her eyes off Cancun. The dapple gray's canter looked more like a gallop for the first few strides, but Jan had eased him back to a more suitable pace by the time they reached the first fence, a line of barrels laid on their sides, with the farm's name printed on them. Cancun pricked his ears at the fence and sailed over easily.

"One down, lots to go," Kyle commented.

"Yeah." Haley held her breath as Cancun neared the second obstacle, a coop. Once again the horse jumped it easily, and Haley started to relax a little. "So far, so good . . . ," she murmured.

The next few jumps went fine too. Then the course turned and wound partway up the hill, passing close to the spot where they were sitting. Haley glanced at the nearest obstacle, an attractive brush jump, and wished she'd brought her camera. It would be fun to get a picture of Cancun sailing over it.

She forgot about that as she heard a murmur rise from the spectators. Glancing back to the horse and rider, she saw that Jan was having trouble. The gray gelding was flinging his head and skittering to one side as they approached the brush.

"Oh no," Haley said, realizing what must have been bothering Cancun. "The cows!"

She glanced over her shoulder at the herd, which was grazing peacefully just a few yards from the fence. Cancun had seen them too, and clearly didn't want to get too close.

Haley held her breath as Jan growled and booted the

horse forward. Instead of cantering on, though, Cancun planted his feet and bucked hard.

Haley gasped along with everyone else. But somehow Jan stayed on, circling Cancun away from the cows and then back again to the line for the brush jump. Cancun didn't buck this time, but he stopped and backed up several strides out.

"Yikes," Haley said. "He's really scared."

"Yeah." Andrew sounded worried.

Jan stopped her horse and gave him a rub on the neck. Then she urged him forward again at a walk. He hesitated but did as she asked, keeping a wary eye on the cows. Jan walked him back and forth, getting closer each time, then stopped and patted him. Glancing at the jump judge by the brush, she raised her hand, then rode over to talk to the woman.

"Wait, what's she doing?" Haley said.

Kyle shrugged. "Retiring, looks like."

"What?" Haley couldn't believe it.

But it seemed to be true—Jan was talking to the jump judge, who pulled out her walkie-talkie and called someone. Haley and the others were too far away to hear what Jan and the judge were saying, but after a bit more discussion Jan nodded and rode off at a trot, passing the brush fence without even trying to jump it.

"Why did she do that?" Haley said. "Cancun was calming down—I'm sure she could've gotten him over the brush and the ditch after it. Then they'd be away from the cows again and everything would be fine. Even with a refusal and some time faults, she might still have finished up okay."

"She isn't doing this for a ribbon," Andrew reminded her. "She's training Cancun, remember? The only thing she cares about is giving him a good experience his first time out. And if she'd pushed it with the cow thing, well . . ."

Haley frowned, but she realized he had a point. "Still, it's too bad." She watched Jan and Cancun, who were close to the end of the course by now. They stopped beside fence thirteen, an inviting roll top, and Jan spoke to the judge there. A moment later she circled around, sent Cancun into an easy canter, and popped him over the jump.

"Good," Andrew said. "See, she ended the course on a good note."

Haley nodded and checked her watch, realizing she needed to go get Wings tacked up soon for her own round.

She still thought it was too bad that her trainer had decided to retire on course, but suddenly she realized there was a silver lining.

With Jan out, that means we're definitely riding to win! Haley thought with a shiver of anticipation as she slid down from the fence and hurried toward the trailer.

Before Haley knew it, her ride time was almost there. She and Wings had had a good warm-up and were waiting near the start box when Riley rode into view. The older girl was starting two riders ahead of Haley, and Haley was glad she'd get to see Riley's first few fences.

That way I'll have a better sense of how much we need to do to beat her, she thought, smiling at Riley as the older girl rode past.

Riley didn't seem to notice her. She had her hands full—Athena was on her toes, snorting and jigging as they approached the start box.

"Wow, she looks tense," Haley murmured, patting Wings, who was alert but calm as they waited.

Moments later Athena trotted out of the start box,

skittering sideways a few strides, before Riley got her cantering toward the first fence. The mare took off from an awkward short spot but still cleared the barrels with at least a foot to spare. The next jump, the coop, went better; Athena met it out of stride and jumped cleanly and quickly.

Wings was getting restless, so Haley circled him. When she came back around, she was just in time to see Riley and Athena's approach to the next obstacle, a double hanging log at maximum height. Haley thought that jump was one of the most imposing on the course—it was big and solid and dark, set on a slight uphill approach that made it look even bigger. It looked as if Athena didn't like the looks of it either. The mare was tossing her head, seeming agitated and trying to veer out to one side. But Riley kept her going, and their approach to the logs looked pretty good—until a large bird suddenly flew up from some tall weeds nearby with a flurry of wings.

The big mare spooked and spun, then let out a hard buck—flinging Riley headfirst into the solid jump.

• CHAPTER •
11

"OH NO!" HALEY BLURTED OUT, CLUTCHING her reins so tightly that Wings backed up a few steps. People were pouring toward Riley from all directions. The jump judge was at the girl's side in seconds, kneeling down beside her still form.

Please be okay, please be okay, Haley chanted in her head.

"Hold on course!" the man running the start box yelled, though Haley didn't know why he'd bothered—it was pretty obvious to everyone.

"Loose horse!" someone else shouted.

Again, that seemed obvious. But a second later Haley saw Athena galloping in her direction with her reins trailing and stirrups flapping. Haley had been so focused on Riley that she'd lost track of the mare for a second, but it looked as if Athena was still pretty freaked out. A few people darted out and tried to grab her or head her off, but Athena dodged them all easily and kept going, charging up the slight hill in the direction of the start box and the trailers beyond. Haley gulped, picturing the carnage the panicked mare could cause to herself and others in the crowded, cluttered parking area.

"Come on, boy—get up!" Haley didn't stop to think as she booted Wings into a canter, heading to cut Athena off from the quickest path to the trailers.

The rider waiting to go just before her, a young woman on a compact little bay gelding, caught on quickly. She sent her horse out as well, angling to block Athena's escape in the other direction.

Athena saw them coming and slowed slightly, veering suddenly off to the right. Haley didn't even have to tell Wings what to do—he spun to cut her off, head lowered and ears flattened.

Just like when we're chasing cows, Haley thought with a small smile.

"Send her this way!" the other rider hollered.

Haley nodded, sending her pony spurting forward to turn the bigger horse back toward the bay gelding. Athena broke to a trot as she headed in that direction, then suddenly stopped and spun over her hocks like a reining horse.

Haley pushed Wings forward, leaning out of her saddle as far as she could. She held her breath and grabbed for the mare's swinging reins, letting out a gasp of relief as her fingers closed around them.

"Gotcha!" she cried, sitting up and back in case the mare tried to pull away.

But now that Athena had been caught, the horse's panic seemed to leave her all at once. The big mare's head dropped, and she let out a long sigh.

One of the volunteers from the start box jogged over. "Thanks for catching her. That was great," the woman exclaimed. "I can take her back to the trailers, have the vet take a look just in case."

Haley handed over the reins. She patted Wings on the neck, proud of him for doing what needed to be done.

"Come on," she told him. "Let's go see if Riley's okay."

She kicked him into a trot, and then slowed to a walk when they neared the crowd by the log fence. Tracey spotted her coming and hurried to meet her.

"Oh wow, that was crazy!" she exclaimed. "Good thing Owen and Vance know first aid."

"Huh?" Haley stood in her stirrups to peer over the heads of the crowd. She was relieved to see that Riley was sitting up, though she was leaning against the jump and looked pretty dazed. The two boys were kneeling on either side of her.

"Where's my horse?" Riley's weak voice drifted toward Haley on the breeze. "Is she okay?"

"Don't try to talk," Vance told her. "I'm sure your horse is fine."

Haley jumped down from the saddle and tossed the reins at a surprised Tracey. "Here, hold him a sec," she ordered. Then she pushed her way through the crowd.

"Athena?" Riley was saying, struggling to sit up straighter. "Where'd she go?"

"Seriously, don't do that, okay?" Owen said, putting a

hand on the girl's shoulder. "The doctor's coming."

"We got her, Riley," Haley blurted out when she reached them. "Athena's fine. Someone's taking her back to the trailers right now."

Riley slumped and sighed. "Good," she whispered. "Thanks, um . . ." She blinked, looking confused.

"Haley," Haley supplied. "And you're welcome." She hesitated. "Um, listen, I'm sorry about what happened. Especially since you were probably going to win."

The last few words almost stuck in her throat. But she had to say them—they were the truth.

A ghost of a smile flitted across Riley's pale face. "Thanks," she said again. "But, you know—that's eventing for you. Anyway, I probably should've withdrawn after dressage. I could tell Athena wasn't herself today."

"Really?" Haley remembered what Kyle had said about Riley having trouble in dressage.

"Yeah. But I figured I could ride through it." Riley sighed. "Obviously not." Her eyes met Haley's, and she tried again to smile. "Guess today was my day for bad luck, like yours last time, huh?"

Haley didn't know how to answer that. Bad luck? Was that what Riley thought had caused Haley's fall last time?

"Anyway, good luck with that cute pony today," Riley said, her voice so soft now that it was hard to hear. "Hope this doesn't throw you off, but I can tell you guys are a great team."

"Oh—thanks!" Haley said in surprise. "I, um . . ."

"Excuse me, coming through." A man carrying a black leather bag with a red cross on it pushed his way between Emma and another spectator. "Doctor, coming through, please."

Owen and Vance stepped back. Owen said a few words to the doctor, who nodded.

"Thanks, young man," he said. Then he kneeled beside Riley.

Owen walked over to Haley. "You okay?" he asked. "That was kind of scary."

Haley didn't answer. She was still thinking about what Riley had said. Luck? *Could* it really just have been bad luck that had struck her and Wings last time? It wasn't as if Haley had figured out any other way to explain it. Still, this sport was all about preparation, boldness, athleticism. How could luck possibly play such a big part?

"Haley?" Owen poked her in the shoulder. "You there?"

She blinked at him, then swatted his hand away. "Yeah, I'm here." She turned and looked for Tracey and Wings, squaring her shoulders with determination. "I've got to go find Wings and get ready to ride."

"You sure about this?" Jan squinted up at Haley, who was back in the saddle watching the young woman on the bay gelding ride out of the start box. The EMTs had taken Riley away to the hospital to x-ray her ribs and shoulder and check for a concussion, and now the event was back under way.

Haley's eyes followed the young woman on the bay horse, watching them leap easily over the first jump.

"Yeah," she said. "I'm sure. I want to go."

Jan slid her hand under Wings's girth, making sure it was snug. "Okay. I'm just saying, there's no shame in withdrawing after witnessing a fall like that."

"I know. But I'm okay." Haley shortened her reins as the starter glanced her way. "I'd better get over there."

"All right. Good luck."

Haley winced at the word "luck." She still didn't know how to feel about what Riley had said. But she could worry about that later. Right now she had a course to ride.

Soon she and Wings were in the start box, and the starter was counting down to her time. ". . . three, two, one—good luck!" the man called.

When Haley released Wings, he trotted out of the start box and burst into a canter. Feeling a twinge of alarm, Haley sat back, squeezing the reins.

"Easy, boy," she said. "Not too fast."

Wings shook his head as they approached the barrel jump, clearly not liking her tight hold. But Haley knew he could clear the barrels from a trot if he had to—a slow canter to the short spot would do just fine.

When they got there, Wings hurled himself over the barrels and opened up his stride on the far side. Once again Haley slowed him down, eyeing the coop a dozen strides ahead. When Haley had walked the course earlier, she had seen that the approach was a little tricky, and she wanted to be sure she didn't miscalculate.

Once again Wings cleared the obstacle easily. Haley eased him around the curve, collecting his stride as the course sloped uphill. Her heart thumped when she saw the double log jump looming ahead.

We can do this, she told herself firmly. *We can do it, we can do it. . . .*

She didn't even realize she'd been holding her breath until they landed and cantered away on the far side of the logs. Letting her breath out with a whoosh, she smiled.

Then she gasped as something squawked loudly and burst into motion off to her left. It was a bird! Maybe even the same one that had spooked Athena.

Wings reacted quickly, leaping to one side and snorting. Haley froze, the next few seconds zipping through her mind like a movie in fast motion—herself flying through the air like Riley, landing headfirst on the hard ground . . .

But no. Haley had lost her stirrups and was a little crooked, but she was still in the saddle. And Wings had already recovered; he was cantering on, ears pricked toward the log-cabin-shaped jump that came next.

Haley quickly fished for her stirrups, heart pounding with adrenaline and head throbbing with uncertainty. That had been close! And now they'd be at the cabin in a few more strides. She needed to act fast if she wanted to pull up—withdraw, regroup, try again another day. . . .

But she couldn't do it. Her pony was galloping on to meet the jump, brave and strong and ready. Why would they stop now?

"Go on, Wings," she whispered, giving a squeeze with her calves and then leaning forward as he sailed over the cabin.

She was smiling when they landed, her usual confidence already coming back. Turning her head, she looked for their next jump.

◆ CHAPTER ◆
12

HALEY WAS STILL SMILING A COUPLE OF hours later as she and Wings cleared the last fence in their stadium jumping round. They'd just ridden a clean round to go with the one they'd turned in earlier on cross-country. Her friends were all cheering at the gate as she rode out of the ring.

"That was awesome, Hales!" Tracey exclaimed.

"Yeah," Emma added. "You're, like, ready for the Olympics!"

"Great job, Haley," Kyle added, stepping forward to give Wings a pat. "That should move you up a place or two."

Haley noticed that Owen was clapping along with the

others. He caught her eye and grinned. "Yeah, not bad for a sissy English rider," he said.

Haley frowned slightly. Would he ever get over that?

"But Wings here might just make a good Western horse after all," Owen added. He nudged Vance with his shoulder. "Did you hear how he rounded up that loose horse like a real cow pony?"

"Uh-huh." Vance nodded. "We'd better watch out for him at the next penning, huh?"

Haley's smile returned. Okay, maybe Owen and his friends would always think Western riding was better than eventing. But at least now they appreciated Wings a little more. She'd take it.

Jan appeared, grabbing Wings by the bridle. "Out of the way, everyone," she said briskly. "Let's get this awesome jumping cow pony back and give him a bath and some pampering now that he's done for the day."

"Yeah." Haley dropped her reins and leaned forward to hug her pony, not minding a bit that he was kind of sweaty. "He totally earned it!"

◆ ◆ ◆

Haley was combing out her pony's wet mane when Kyle came running toward her. Right behind him was Andrew, followed by Haley's school friends.

"Results are up!" Kyle reported breathlessly, skidding to a stop. "Guess what? Augie and I actually got a ribbon!"

"Really?" Haley dropped the comb into her bucket and clapped her hands. "That's awesome! Congratulations!"

"Thanks." Kyle grinned sheepishly. "Only eighth place, and only elementary, but still."

Andrew had caught up by now. He clapped Kyle on the back. "That's great," he said. "Especially since one of the horses that beat you probably cost more than both our houses put together."

"Dragon?" Haley guessed.

Andrew nodded. "Claire won the elementary division."

"Surprise, surprise," Kyle said. "Anyway, Haley, you finished sixth in BN."

Haley nodded, glancing at Andrew. "How'd you and Turbo do?"

"Third," he said, suddenly sounding shy. "I'm really proud of him."

"You should be." Haley smiled. "That's amazing. Congrats."

Tracey stepped forward and slung her arm around Haley's shoulders. "Well, I think you should've won, Hales. Are you totally bummed?"

Haley winced, remembering all her talk about winning lately. "No, it's fine," she said quickly. "Okay, so maybe it's true that I came into this hoping to win. But I realized that's not the most important thing, you know?"

"Really?" Vance leaned against Jan's trailer, playing with Wings's lips as the pony snuffled at him. "Seems pretty important to me."

"Don't get me wrong—I'm not saying I wouldn't have loved to win that blue ribbon," Haley said. "And maybe next time we will. Or maybe it'll be the time after that." She shrugged. "Who knows. As long as Wingsie and I have fun, keep getting better, and come back safe, it's all good."

"Spoken like a weenie English rider," Owen joked. His voice shifted into a goofy falsetto. "'Oh, I don't care if I win. It's an honor just to be here.'"

Vance stepped forward and gave him a shove. "Cut it out, dude."

"Yeah, stuff it, Owen." Tracey glared at him. "Haley's being, like, totally sincere here, okay?"

Emma patted Haley on the arm. "Don't pay any attention to him, Haley. I know exactly what you mean."

"Hey, I was just kidding around," Owen protested, his eyes darting around at all of them but not quite meeting Haley's glare. "Look, I'll make it up to you. How about some sodas? I'll go buy us some."

Without waiting for a response, he dashed off in the direction of the concessions stands near the jumping ring. Meanwhile Tracey squeezed Haley's shoulders again and leaned closer.

"Did you see that?" she whispered excitedly into her ear. "His face was totally turning red. That *so* means he likes you, Hales!"

Haley pushed her away. She didn't want to talk about Owen right now. Because she was starting to realize that having him here hadn't been that bad after all. Maybe it had even been kind of . . . nice. But that thought just made her confused, and she didn't really want to think about it.

"Come on, guys," she said to Kyle and Andrew. "Let's go find out when they're handing over our ribbons."

It was fully dark by the time Haley finished settling Wings into his stall for the night. When she emerged from the barn, yawning and looking forward to a shower and her soft bed, Bandit was sitting beneath the floodlight shining over the barnyard.

"Hey, boy," Haley said, and whistled.

The dog pricked his ears at her but stayed where he was. Haley blinked in surprise.

"Yo, Bandit," she said, patting her knees. "Come here, boy. Don't you want to say hi?"

Finally the dog leaped up and trotted over, tail wagging slowly. Haley was a little worried when she realized he hadn't been there to meet her when she'd first arrived with Wings. Was he sick or something?

But Bandit looked perfectly healthy as he pressed himself against her legs. Haley thought back over the past week or two, trying to remember if she'd noticed anything strange about his behavior. He'd seemed perfectly normal the first couple of times she'd worked on his training, though he'd been a little odd after that, sometimes darting away after just a few minutes of sits and stays. . . .

"Oh, Bandit," she blurted out, suddenly realizing what was wrong. "I guess I've been a little intense about the whole training thing lately, huh? And not just with Wings." She dropped to her knees, wrapping the wiggly, angular dog in a big hug.

She smiled as she felt his tongue slurp over her cheek. Bandit would forgive her—he always did.

"Sorry, buddy," she whispered into his warm, furry body. "I'm still going to work on your obedience to try to keep you safe. But we'll be sure to make the training a little more fun from now on, okay?"

She spent a few minutes tossing a stick for her furry friend. But when she couldn't stop yawning, she gave him one last head rub and headed inside.

Moments later she was in her room logging on to the Pony Post. She'd promised to update her friends after the event, and she wanted to be sure to post the photos that

Tracey had taken with the fancy smartphone she'd gotten recently as a hand-me-down from her sister. Tracey had already forwarded the pictures to Haley's e-mail.

Haley uploaded the photos first. Then she opened a text box and quickly described the event, from her iffy dressage performance, to Riley's fall, to the final placings. She also told them that someone had reported back that Riley had suffered a mild concussion and bruised ribs, along with plenty of scrapes and bruises. But she'd be able to ride again as soon as the doctors said her head had had enough time to heal.

Haley posted that much and then read it over, checking to be sure she hadn't forgotten anything important. Then she sat back, trying to decide how to say what she wanted to tell them next. Finally she began to type again.

[HALEY] So you're probably wondering if I'm disappointed that we didn't win, right? Lol, I don't blame u—it's all I've been talking about. But I think u guys sort of guessed what was happening before

I did. I was getting too intense again, sorta like

before that clinic. Only this time it was all about

winning, instead of just trying to get everything

done. And I know now that being like that isn't so

cool. I mean, there's nothing wrong w/doing your

best and wanting to win. But u can take that too far,

u know?

She sent that much and stopped to think again. Her sixth-place ribbon was on the desk where she'd tossed it, and she smiled when she saw it, knowing she'd never forget today. No blue ribbon could change that.

[HALEY] I def. don't want to end up like that girl

Claire I just told u about. I mean, she's so obsessed

w/winning that she traded in her perfectly nice

horse in search of victory, even tho it was her

own riding that hurt her last time. Crazy!!! I guess it

worked, tho, since she won this time. But I'd rather

never win another ribbon in my life than trade in my

awesome Wings!!!!!!!!!!!

She sent that message too. When it appeared, she remembered something else she'd wanted to say.

> [HALEY] Besides, I realized u can do everything u
>
> can think of to make sure u win, and u still might
>
> have bad luck and lose. So why not have fun
>
> either way?

She smiled as she posted that message, but part of her still felt a little troubled by the idea that luck could have such a big effect on eventing—and on life. No matter how prepared you were, something unexpected could come along and mess you up big-time. Her mind wandered back to Riley for a second, and the bad luck of that bird flying out at just the wrong time. And that wasn't the only bad luck that had come into play today. If the event hadn't been located right next to a cow pasture—or even if the cows had decided to graze at the opposite end of their pasture—maybe Jan wouldn't have had to withdraw, and maybe Augie wouldn't have been distracted and made Haley rush her warm-up, and maybe their dressage score would have been good enough to move them up into the top ribbons. . . .

Maybe, maybe, maybe, she thought with a shake of her head. *I guess we'll never know, though. Which is sort of the point.*

Realizing that her eyes were drooping shut of their own accord, she smothered another yawn and opened one last text box.

[HALEY] Anyway, it was an interesting day, so it's all good. Not that I won't try to win next time out, lol—I'm still me, and I still like to win! But winning isn't the only reason I do this, right? It's not even the main one. Anyway, thanks for trying to let me know I was getting too intense. Maybe I didn't listen, ha ha, but it's nice to know that u guys are always there for me, just like I'm always here for all of u. Can't wait to hear what fun things you and yr amazing ponies do next!!! But it'll have to wait until tmw, lol, b/c I'm beat. Good night!

◆ Glossary ◆

beginner novice: A level of eventing. The sport is divided into six recognized levels. From lowest to highest they are beginner novice, novice, training, preliminary, intermediate, and advanced. (Advanced-level eventers are the ones you see competing in the Olympic Games.) There are also many local, unrecognized events that feature levels below beginner novice, which can be useful for riders and horses new to eventing. These low levels can have names such as elementary, introductory, starter, tadpole, grasshopper, and various others.

combined training: Another name for eventing.

free lease: The lease of a horse or pony for which no lease fee is paid. Sometimes also referred to as a "feed lease," since the leaser frequently (but not always) pays for the animal's feed, farrier, and other basic expenses during the course of the lease.

hocks: A joint in the rear leg of a horse or pony. While located about halfway down the leg (roughly parallel to the knees of the horse's front legs), the hock corresponds biologically to the ankle of a human leg.

jump judge: In the cross-country phase of eventing, a judge is posted at each obstacle on the course. These judges are often volunteers. Each judge is responsible for scoring at his or her fence, confirming whether a horse and rider made it over, and noting any penalties, such as refusals or falls.

quarter horse: The nickname of the American quarter horse, a versatile breed of horse developed in the early days of the United States. The American quarter horse is the most popular breed in the US today, and its breed association is the largest in the world.

roping: A rodeo event in which two riders must rope and tie a steer. It's the only rodeo event in which men and women commonly compete against each other.

start box: The spot where a horse and rider begin their cross-country course. This is often a three-sided, fenced-in "box" about the size of a large stall.

stock horse: A type of horse suited for working with livestock. Quarter horses, paints, and Appaloosas are the most common American stock horses.

transitions: Changing from one gait (or halt) to another. Upward transitions are from a slower gait to a faster one. For instance a rider can do a transition from walk to trot, from halt to canter, and various others. A downward transition is from a faster gait to a slower one—for instance from gallop to canter, from trot to halt, and various others.

Marguerite Henry's Ponies of Chincoteague
is inspired by the award-winning books by Marguerite
Henry, the beloved author of such classic horse stories as
King of the Wind; *Misty of Chincoteague*; *Justin Morgan Had
a Horse*; *Stormy, Misty's Foal*; *Misty's Twilight*; and *Album
of Horses*, among many other titles.

Learn more about the world of Marguerite Henry at
www.MistyofChincoteague.org.

Don't miss the next book in the series!

Book 8: *The Road Home*

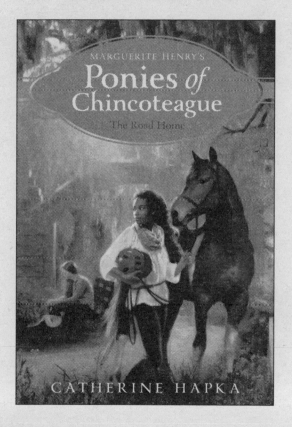

Saddle up for a new world of classic horse tales!

For a full round-up of pony stories inspired by Marguerite Henry's *Misty of Chincoteague* visit **PoniesOfChincoteague.com**!

Simon & Schuster Children's Publishing · A CBS COMPANY

ALADDIN